More love stories by Amanda Hamm

LOVE IN ANDAUK
EVERYTHING OLD (BOOK 1)
INTO THE FIRE (BOOK 2)
BY ITS COVER (BOOK 3)
WHAT GOES AROUND (BOOK 4)

THEY SEE A FAMILY
THE STUDY GROUP (EBOOK NOVELLA)

COFFEE AND DONUTS
SAID AND UNSAID (BOOK 1)
SOFIE WAITS (BOOK 2)
A PERFECTLY GOOD MAN (BOOK 3)
NOT COMPLICATED (BOOK 4)

STORIES FROM HARTFORD
ANDREW'S KEY (BOOK 1)
JEALOUSY & YAMS (BOOK 2)
COLLECTING ZEBRAS (BOOK 3)
THE CHRISTMAS PROJECT (BOOK 4)
HEARTS ON THE WINDOW (EBOOK NOVELLA)

MEET CUTE: 5 ROMANTIC SHORT STORIES

THE 4TH FLOOR LOUNGE

The Art of Patience

Romance Arts
Book 2

Amanda Hamm

ISBN: 978-1-943598-15-1

1

The beep that signaled successfully clocking out was highly satisfying. Audra took off her apron and wadded it up.

"Big plans for the weekend?" asked a coworker who was just beginning her shift. The woman's tone was skeptical.

Audra shrugged. It was Friday, and she was excited about having some friends over for a game that night. Too excited to let it be used as fodder for a joke. "Not too much," she said.

"Same old, same old?" The woman smiled mockingly. "Twelve hours of prayer, lots of sacrifice... hey, maybe you'll get a vision. That'd almost be entertainment."

"Be nice," a male voice admonished.

Audra tried not to groan out loud at the arrival of her defender.

The woman rolled her eyes. "Save your breath. You're not getting anywhere with Miss Holier Than Thou." She walked away, leaving Audra with the guy who thought he was charming and the exit that was behind him.

"I like that necklace," he said. "Much prettier than the one with the dead guy."

Audra forced a smile. She was wearing a plain cross instead of a crucifix. "Have a nice night," she said.

"You, too." He stepped aside enough for her to leave but was still too close.

Freedom felt good, even in a car that had been sitting in the sun. Audra blasted the air conditioning and turned the radio up loud enough to hear over the rushing wind. She sang along. The drive was short enough that she only heard a few songs before parking in front of her house.

She showered to remove the work smell and put on a pair of shorts and a top in a shade of cheerful pink. Violet wouldn't be home for almost two hours. That wasn't enough time to paint. But it was enough time to dream of painting.

There was so much more room in Audra's closet now that half her paintings were on display in town. She couldn't wait to fill it up again. She opened the sketchbook on her bed, ready for any ideas she might want to write down. Then she began to stare at each finished painting in turn. Where had her thoughts drifted before the final picture? Had there been any side paths she wanted to explore later?

Purple flowers held her attention the longest. She remembered a crazy idea about putting a tiny face in the center of one of the flowers. How could a face not look happy surrounded by bright petals? It didn't. It looked creepy and disturbing. Audra had scraped that paint off fast. She'd had other ideas though, different angles to try. She could always paint more flowers.

The front door opened. What happened to the two hours? Audra set the canvas down and hurried out to greet her roommate. "Dinner!" she said.

Violet laughed and said, "I'll help as soon as I drop this." She held up a purse.

"Meet me in the kitchen." The kitchen was part of the living room but separated by some lower cabinets. A table straddled the space. They didn't need a six-person table for two people, but it had been a gift from Violet's parents. Audra believed a free table could have six chairs if it wanted to. She scooted around it and grabbed a bag of fish fillets from the freezer. Violet followed in a minute, washed her hands and began to study the recipe while Audra peeled the wraps off the fish.

"Uh… did you read this recipe?"

"I skimmed it," Audra said.

"The tilapia is supposed to be thawed first."

Audra spun around, still holding a solid piece of fish in one hand. "Is that a problem?"

"You're the one who works at a restaurant," Violet observed.

"I don't cook."

Violet cracked a smile, and Audra laughed at herself before anyone could say anything about how that was obvious.

The cold was beginning to sting Audra's fingers. She pulled off the rest of the plastic and dropped the fish into the pan. "I usually put it in the oven still frozen," she said.

"But you usually make it by itself," Violet said. "It'll take longer than… the rice might burn by the time the fish is done."

"Can we do the rice in a separate pan, then put them together?"

"Probably." Violet got out a different pan. "It might have been better not to try a new recipe when we're expecting company."

"You're the one who wanted something fancy."

"I only said we should look like we used a recipe, which we almost are," Violet said. "We'll make it work."

They did. Mostly. Elaine and Alison came over in time to see Audra spooning the rice around the fish so she admitted they had to make some last-minute adjustments. The visitors complimented the food anyway. It was a fairly civilized meal. Elaine was meeting Violet for the first time. She asked some background questions while they ate and kept up conversation as she and Alison helped clear the table. She asked if one of them had advertised for a roommate or if Violet and Audra had been friends a long time.

"Something in between," Audra said.

"We were randomly assigned as roommates in college," Violet explained. "We got along really well so when we both decided not to continue school, it seemed like a good idea to at least continue sharing a place. And the cost of one."

Elaine nodded. "I love this big house. Are your neighbors ever an issue?"

It was a really big old house that had been converted into several apartments. Audra's brothers, Ryan and Trevor, lived in one of the apartments so she suppressed a grin at the suggestion of her neighbors being an issue. She knew that wasn't what Elaine meant. "No, either the walls are thick enough or everyone is quiet."

"No one has complained about us either," Violet added. She had brought the box of cards to the table. "Are we ready to play?"

"Yes," Alison said. "I think so."

"You're going to be patient if we misinterpreted anything, right?" Elaine asked.

"Of course." Violet began to deal.

The guests had been learning to play on their own. It was a four-person game, and there were two of them. They were bound to need advice just being novices anyway. The seats they had chosen for dinner made Violet and Alison a team and paired Audra with Elaine. It seemed fair to split the more experienced players so they didn't rearrange.

Elaine began the game by passing the dog card to Audra. That was the first point she wanted to clarify. As soon as the opportunity arose, she explained that because the card could be difficult to get rid of, it was better passed to an opponent. She tried to explain that concept again a few hands later.

Elaine had never played before, but the woman had ears, right? How many times had Audra said that giving your partner the dog was generally a bad idea? At least as far as Audra was concerned. Yet Elaine had passed her the dog again. Audra didn't try to clarify her opinion again. The game was almost over anyway. Violet and Alison only needed twenty points to win.

The hand and the game ended. Audra shoved her leftover cards, with that dog, towards Violet. "Let's go check on the guys," she said.

Violet gathered the Tichu cards to put in the box at her elbow. "I thought we were staying here tonight."

Audra felt restless. The guys she meant included both of her brothers and two of their friends, Logan and Cameron. The four guys played Tichu on Friday nights regularly. This was the first week Audra had enough women for her own game. She was happy about that but already missed stopping in to observe the guys' game. She kind of wanted to have her cake and eat it, too. "It's too early to call it a night," she said, "and too late for another game, right?"

Violet shrugged.

Alison looked at Elaine, who was her mom and who would be riding home with her.

"I'm probably too old to play another game tonight," Elaine said. "Need to save some energy for next week."

Audra moved towards her door and said, "Come on." The others shouldn't be difficult to convince. Violet had come lots of times before. She already knew the guys. And Alison had just started dating Trevor.

"Wait a minute," Violet said. She set the box of cards on a shelf and slipped into her bedroom.

"It's still strange to me that your walls are bare," Alison observed. "It seems like an artist should be surrounded by art."

Audra had met Alison and her mom when they agreed to show some of her paintings in their vintage furniture store in town. "I can't hang them all up, and I wouldn't know which ones to choose. Plus, I'm not a real artist."

"You are." Elaine launched into a speech about how having Audra's work in her shop was inspirational. Alison agreed.

Audra decided not to disagree with her new friends out loud.

Why would she want to risk talking them out of selling her work anyway?

"Thanks for waiting," Violet said as she reappeared. She'd fixed her hair. It hadn't been broken of course. Violet had dark, very curly hair. Audra had straight blonde hair. They sometimes laughed about how they both had occasional envy of the other. Audra sometimes wished her hair had more life. It simply hung on her back, flat and boring. Violet thought her hair sometimes had too much life. The curls tangled easily and went everywhere if she worked too hard to separate them. She usually kept the bulk of it pinned to the back of her head with some loose curls dangling. She emerged from her bedroom with it pinned higher and the curls framing her face more.

A sudden thought popped into Audra's head. It was possible that Violet's hair had simply come loose. But it was also possible that she cared about her appearance because of one of the guys they were about to visit. Audra would need to pay attention for other signs of interest.

She led the way around to the side door of the house to Trevor and Ryan's apartment. The door was unlocked. Trevor always tried to give her a hard time about coming in without waiting for him to answer the door when they both knew he left it unlocked so he wouldn't have to get up to answer the door. Audra rang the bell four times before she walked in.

"What in the world was that?" Trevor said.

"I was letting you know that four people were coming in." She grinned at Logan, who had his head down to make his amusement less obvious.

"That's really not how it works," Trevor said, less harsh than usual because he was looking at Alison. "Hi, Alison."

"Hi, Violet," Ryan said.

Cameron silently waved to all of them.

Audra noticed a hint of question in his eyes and realized not everyone in the room knew each other. "Everyone, this is Alison's mom, Elaine Brachy. You know Trevor and Ryan. That's Logan, and that's Cameron." She made her way around the table as she talked and picked up Logan's phone. He always kept the score. "Oh, you guys are close," she said. "You'll probably win after this hand."

"No, we won't," Trevor mumbled.

"Wasn't talking to you," Audra said.

"We can't win if no one's playing." Ryan gestured somewhat impatiently to the trick he'd led.

Once they figured out Logan was the one not paying attention, they finished the hand quickly. It wrapped up the game, and Alison observed that they must play fast since she knew they started later. Audra told her they didn't talk much while they played and would probably have time for another. Logan was already shuffling the cards.

"I guess two of us can get out of your way." Alison waved a hand between her and her mom to show which two she meant. But she looked at Trevor before moving towards the door to ask about their plans for the weekend.

Trevor seemed reluctant to talk to Alison in front of an audience. The solution was so obvious Audra couldn't believe she was the one to have to suggest it. Elaine had done some scheming with Audra and Trevor's grandmother to get Trevor and Alison together. Audra had been enlisted to help. Apparently, the budding relationship still needed some help. "Just take him outside and get it out of him," Audra said. "These guys can wait five minutes." She winked at Elaine, who was already giving her daughter a nudge with her elbow.

Trevor turned slightly pink. A curse of the light skin in their family was that it took only a hint of embarrassment to show up. But he didn't hesitate to stand up and take Alison outside for a private moment.

They were halfway out the door when Elaine called, "You can signal me through the window when you're ready to go."

Audra smiled. The implication that she'd be watching was the kind of thing that was only funny when someone else's mom said it.

"So I hear you'll be taking over next door," Elaine said to Ryan. The Brachys' furniture store was located next to the January Café, which was owned by Audra's grandparents.

Ryan evidently understood that she was talking about his new position as manager there. "Yeah. My first official day is next Saturday."

"Congratulations," Elaine said. "I know May is thrilled to be keeping it in the family."

Audra bit her tongue against pointing out that she was also family.

"Matt, the current manager, said they found a house they like, but they won't close until the end of August so he'll be around to show me the ropes for two or three weeks," Ryan said.

Elaine nodded. "You have a little experience already, am I right?"

"The most basic stuff, yeah," Ryan said. "I worked weekends there my last year of high school."

Audra had worked weekends at the restaurant her last *three* years of high school, and she found the conversation annoying. She went around the table and took Trevor's chair. "I'll stand in for Trevor to choose teams so you can get the cards dealt," she said.

Logan's hands slowed on the cards he was shuffling. "Hmm… guess he probably won't mind that."

"Of course he won't," she said, though she suspected her brother would mind only if someone told him it was her idea.

Logan set his phone in the middle of the table and the three players plus Audra touched a finger to the screen to let the app choose teams. Logan and Ryan needed to switch places for the next game. Somehow Ryan managed to do that while still talking to Elaine about his new job.

Logan leaned in and asked, "Do you wanna deal for him, too?"

Audra answered with a snort. She could tell Logan was kidding both by the tone of his voice and the fact that he'd already begun dealing the cards himself.

"Time to go, Mom," Alison's voice called through the front door as Trevor returned. She waved as Elaine said her goodbyes and exited.

Trevor came up and motioned for Audra to vacate his seat. She'd unconsciously picked up the cards as they landed in front of her, and he didn't say anything about that. He was even smiling a little as she handed them over. Things must have gone pretty well in the few moments he had alone with Alison.

"Nice chat?" Ryan asked.

Trevor shrugged blandly as he kept his eyes on his cards.

It wouldn't be fun to join in the teasing since Audra was genuinely happy for Trevor and Alison, particularly because she felt she had a hand in getting them together. Her Grandma May had been the mastermind, but Audra had played an important role. She was standing between Trevor and Logan. Violet was at the opposite corner between Ryan and Cameron. Audra's mind returned to her suspicion that Violet was interested in one of these guys. Perhaps she could put her newfound matchmaking skills to further use.

The first step would be to figure out which guy had caught her roommate's attention.

"You ladies can grab chairs if you're going to be here for a while." Ryan gestured to a pair of extra chairs against the wall.

Violet looked at Audra in question.

"I think we'll only watch a few hands," Audra said, returning the question with her eyes.

Violet gave a tiny nod of agreement.

"She likes to stand so she can see my cards better anyway,"

Logan said. His tone suggested he was expecting a denial they could all mock. All the guys whined about her looking over their shoulders during a game, but Logan was the only one who didn't hide his cards from her.

Audra didn't bother to deny anything. She preferred to stand for the very reason he'd said. With Trevor in a good mood, she might even be able to peek back and forth between the two hands. She didn't follow as closely as usual with her attention partially on Violet. She was standing behind Ryan, which likely only meant his cards were more visible. She would have a better view of Cameron from there.

Clearly, Trevor could be ruled out. A woman didn't fuss with her appearance for a guy who'd be looking at someone else. There would be no matchmaking potential with someone already attached anyway. Ryan seemed unlikely, though Audra had to admit she'd have trouble seeing romantic potential in her brother. He was the oldest one there, but not by much. He'd finished college three years ahead of the other guys. Logan and Trevor had been friends nearly forever and met Cameron at school. It occurred to Audra that she didn't know where Cameron fit in age order. Age was not a great indicator of compatibility when they were all so close, but Violet and Audra were both twenty-two. If Cameron was the youngest guy, that would make him closest to Violet. That was a place to start.

"Cameron, how old are you?" Audra asked.

He looked up, mildly surprised by the sudden question. "Twenty-four."

"When's your birthday?"

"June."

He'd only recently turned twenty-four, which did make him the youngest. Audra was disappointed the information still wasn't necessarily helpful. Then she returned to the part about him recently turning twenty-four. "Hey. Why didn't you tell anyone when it was your birthday?"

Cameron shrugged. "I think I might have mentioned it."

"Yeah, it wasn't a Friday," Trevor said, "but we said happy birthday or something near it." He seemed to be looking at Ryan and Logan to see if he was remembering right.

Audra rolled her eyes at this lack of acknowledgment, though it didn't surprise her or seem to bother Cameron.

He tossed his last card onto the table. Then his attention seemed to focus more on Audra and what she was asking. "Wait a minute," he said. "Would you have brought me cake if you knew? Because you don't need an excuse."

There were a few chuckles as Ryan nodded hearty agreement. He glanced back to include Violet. "Yeah, if either of you ever wants to bake something before you head over here to watch, we'd do our best to be polite and eat it."

"Absolutely," Logan said.

"Especially if it was brownies," Ryan added.

All four of the guys managed to agree seriously that if they had to eat brownies, they would do their best not to complain.

Audra smiled at the hints as she watched the cards Logan picked up. Trevor had already begun to deal the next hand. In a lot of games, it was impolite to look at your cards before they were all dealt. In Tichu, however, players were allowed to look at the first half of their hands to decide if they wanted to call a Grand Tichu. Audra had never been brave enough for that. Logan had, and he had some pretty good cards. She wondered if he was considering it.

Ryan made a slightly disgusted noise.

Audra glanced over at him. "What?"

"I just accidentally looked at you."

That wasn't nearly as offensive as it would have been if she didn't know what he meant. The guys regularly claimed that she had no poker face, but she was sure she hadn't given anything away.

Logan sighed at her with disappointment, then picked up the rest of his cards. When they traded, she saw that he was given the dog by someone who was not his partner. Audra carefully kept her face from showing that she approved in general or that it was bad for Logan's current hand.

The round ended with Logan and Cameron getting all the points. Audra looked at Violet. "You ready to go?"

"Yeah, I guess." Violet made her way towards the door with a general wave around the table.

A chorus of male voices said, "Good night."

Audra followed Violet as she said, "Good luck."

"Thank you," Trevor said.

"I wasn't talking to you."

He smiled because he already knew that.

The walk around the building was short. Audra slipped off her shoes inside the door. She and Violet would likely go to their separate rooms to prepare for bed soon. But first Audra needed to be sure her matchmaking efforts wouldn't cause friction. "I have a new mission now," she announced.

"Really?" Violet appeared interested.

"Yes," Audra said. But then she didn't know what else to say. How could she find out if Violet would be upset by her plans without spelling out the details or knowing what any of those details were?

Violet put her hands on her hips. "What is your mission?"

"Uh… well, it involves you, but I promise it won't be awkward."

Violet's eyes narrowed in confusion, then they dropped to the ground. "Is it obvious?" She bit the side of her lip waiting for an answer.

Audra didn't take time to gloat over being right. She shook her head vigorously. "Only because I'm super perceptive. Way more so than anyone over there." She motioned towards the apartment they'd just left.

"Good." Violet relaxed and even smiled.

"So I have permission to carry out my mission?"

Confirmation was not immediate. Violet stared at her for a moment looking torn. "What are you going to do?" she asked.

"I don't know," Audra said. "Yet."

Violet actually laughed at the admission. "Okay. When you decide, make sure it isn't… Just don't do or say anything that…" She frowned as she figured out the right words. "I want us to still be able to go over there and watch the games without anyone feeling tense or awkward. Do you think that's possible?"

"Of course," Audra said. She could form her plan around that stipulation. And given that tension and awkwardness would only show up if she failed, there was nothing to worry about.

Violet still seemed a bit worried. But she nodded and said, "Okay. Good night." She did not shake her head or tell Audra she didn't want her to try to meddle.

Audra was energized by getting Violet on board. She almost skipped into her bedroom. It was a little hard to sit still as she picked up her journal. She wrote her prayer intentions for the day. God granting her the perfect idea to turn Violet and Cameron into a happy couple was at the top of her list. Audra chewed on the end of her pen while she pondered where to start. She didn't know Cameron very well, and that might be the key. She needed to probe him for common interests or activities. Delicately, of course.

2

I t was called Next Love. If Logan thought about it, he'd think it was a rather strange name for a furniture store. But he didn't think about it. The store had always been there, right next to the January Café, which was a place he'd been in and out of countless times in his life. He'd never been inside Next Love.

The place sold used furniture that was professionally fixed up to look like new. Logan always assumed that would put it out of his price range. After seeing Alison's custom work, he'd only revised his opinion to think it would be worth it if he was willing to spend that much.

He was on his way to Next Love for the first time, though he was still not in need of expensive furniture. He was going to buy a painting. Maybe. He hoped he was going to buy a painting, but he didn't know if he could truly expect that.

Audra had been painting since high school. Her first efforts were promising, and the latest works brilliant. She did slightly abnormal landscapes. The pictures were pretty, and if you looked at one long enough, you'd spot something a little off. Maybe the flowers in the background were a bit larger than they should have been or the rocks on the shore were balanced in a way that wasn't physically possible. The oddities blended in well enough to make the painting seem typical at a glance. They made everyone who noticed feel as though they were in on a joke. At least that was how Logan felt. And every now and then she painted something that didn't have anything unusual, and he could look at one of those forever trying to figure out how she was messing with his head.

She'd been giving her work to friends and family almost as long as she'd been creating it. Sometimes they even came with instructions on which earlier, and in Audra's opinion lesser, work the new one should replace. At some point, Logan realized he was probably the only person Audra knew who didn't have at least one of her paintings. He'd joked about it for a while, tried to hint that he'd like one. Eventually, he'd asked her directly. She refused to give him one, and she refused to explain why. She even seemed to imply that he should already know why.

He'd offered to buy one, suggested that the paints and canvases he'd given her for Christmases and birthdays might entitle him to a finished product, asked her what the requirements were to merit a painting. She always just said no. She didn't get mad at him, at least not that he could perceive. She didn't tell him to stop asking or explain the circumstances under which he'd ever be allowed to acquire some of her art.

The whole thing was frustrating. The most frustrating part was that he couldn't figure out how Audra felt about it. Was it a game to her, a test to see who could be more stubborn? Had he unknowingly insulted her work at some point? Did she really not want him to have her work, or did she wonder how many times he'd ask?

At any rate, Logan had decided it was time to try again. Now that Audra had her work on display and on sale in public, maybe he could simply walk in like any other customer and buy a painting. He didn't really expect it to be that easy. He hoped he'd at least be showing support even if she rejected it.

Next Love had a large wooden door with a fancy window. Behind the door, Logan discovered a mess. That was the first word that came to mind, though it wasn't as bad as it sounded. There was such a large quantity and variety of furniture that it overwhelmed his eyes at first. Tiny end tables sat next to chests a person could fit inside and tables and dressers and chairs and wood in many shapes and no apparent order.

"Hey!"

Logan turned towards the sound of a friendly female voice, and his eyes focused on Elaine Brachy, otherwise known as Alison's mom.

She snapped her fingers twice with the expression of someone digging up a memory. "Logan, right?"

"Yeah. Hello."

"Hi," she said. "Can I help you with something or would you prefer someone else help you with something?" Her eyes roved towards the back of the narrow shop as she spoke. It wasn't that narrow. It was markedly longer than it was wide though. Audra and Alison were talking farther in, and they both smiled at him.

"I'd like to browse the art," he said. Once he'd gotten over the bombardment of wood, he saw what he recognized as Audra's work along a side wall.

"Be my guest," Elaine said. "It is wonderful."

He nodded in firm agreement before he headed towards that wall to earnestly browse. He wasn't just going to buy a painting, he was going to buy one he liked. Well, he liked most of them. He still intended to approach it as a serious decision. He couldn't afford even an appearance of patronization after all this time. Some of the paintings were familiar. Audra occasionally brought newly finished work when she interrupted their Friday Tichu nights.

The younger women were both watching him so he thought he should say hello before he spent too much time studying the art. He moved past most of it with only quick glances. "Hi, Audra. Hi, Alison."

"Hello." They said the word in unison with a surprisingly musical quality, then smiled at each other. Either they were amused by the unplanned, two-note concert or by something they were talking about before Logan arrived. It was probably the notes.

"I've never been in here before," he said. "There doesn't seem to be a lot of... organization."

"Yeah, I know," Alison said. "We talk about trying a new system now and then but can never... My dad thinks we should have sections for different types of furniture, and my mom thinks we should try to group pieces that might go well together. I kind of agree with both of them but not enough to... We spend a lot of time moving furniture as it is. If we were trying to do anything other than put it where it fits, that would be real fun."

Audra smiled at her dry tone.

It made Logan smile as well, but Audra's was more noteworthy.

"So what brings you in today?" Alison asked.

"Yeah. What brings you in?" Audra repeated the question before he could answer it, which gave him a few extra seconds to decide *how* to answer it.

And he wasted those seconds noticing some contrasts. First, the same question was posed very differently. Alison asked in a friendly, relaxed manner, while Audra's words had an undercurrent of suspicion. Alison wore jeans and a t-shirt with an assortment of stains that seemed to have been acquired over many projects. But her hair was in a neat ponytail with a ribbon so she didn't look sloppy or careless. Dedicated was a better adjective. Someone who got too focused on work to worry what happened to her clothes.

Logan noticed all that mostly because Audra, who worked with paint on a regular basis, never had any paint on her. Not even under her fingernails. She looked great in a spotless dress. She usually wore dresses only to church, but he supposed it made sense she'd want to impress potential customers. The thought reminded him why he was there and that both women were waiting for him to explain why he was there.

Was Audra less likely to refuse to sell to him in front of Alison? Doubtful. Would she feel pressured into it and then regret it? Also doubtful. Did Alison already know what Logan could never find out? He had no idea. It might be best not to lead with sales talk. "Audra's been talking about having her work on display," he said. "I wanted to see for myself."

"You know not to touch it, right?" Alison said. "I'd hate for her to hurt you with that pocket level."

Logan laughed because he knew she was teasing Audra, who was kind of obsessed with keeping her paintings straight.

Audra sent an elbow into Alison's ribs.

"Ow!" Alison doubled over in fake pain – it was a very light jab – and said, "See! She even hurts people who joke about tilting her paintings."

"You're fine," Audra said.

Alison stood up smiling. "Okay, well, I do have a few things I should be working on so I'll leave Audra to be your tour guide." She took a few steps to what seemed to be her work area and put her hands on her hips as though trying to remember where she left off.

Logan turned back to Audra, who was still eyeing him suspiciously. "This is really cool," he said with a wave towards her work on the wall.

"It is." She was smiling but clearly trying to fight it. "I mean, I always thought that if my work was on display somewhere, it would only be after years and years of trying to sell it on my own and writing pleading letters to galleries and that seemed like a huge long shot. I never really expected it. And this is even better." Her smile faded. "But why are you really here?"

"Am I not allowed to look at the art?"

She shrugged. "You can look."

There was definitely an implication that some things would not be allowed, but Logan wasn't ready to cross that bridge. He hadn't decided which one he wanted. "I don't think I've seen this one before." He pointed to a nearby painting. It was a waterfall, not a spectacular deluge like Niagara but a narrow strip of water down the right side of the canvas. There were some boulders it splashed over and plenty of wildflowers. It was energizing somehow. The colors, the moving water, the overall scene made him want to run around and... it made him imagine kicking the tops off those flowers. Audra might not appreciate that thought. He studied the details to figure out what she'd done to make it unique.

Were the splashes too high or too low or on the wrong side of the rocks? That all seemed natural. What about the flowers? Did those normally grow in clumps? She'd used mostly purple, white and yellow and those didn't seem unusual for wildflowers.

Audra was waiting happily as he stared at her work. Was she growing amused because she knew what he couldn't find or because he was trying to find something that wasn't there?

Logan swept his eyes over the clear sky, no real clouds but hints of white. It happened to look a lot like the sky he'd seen on his way in. "I give up," he said. "Am I missing something or not?"

"Whew, I pass," she said.

"You pass?" Logan had felt as though he was the one being tested.

"Yeah, that's not a kooky one," Audra said. Her grandpa lovingly called her altered reality paintings kooky, and she'd taken over the word as an honored descriptor. "Sometimes when people study the normal ones, I'm afraid they'll point out something is too big or the wrong color or... and then I'll have to admit I didn't do it on purpose."

Logan held in his laugh because she appeared serious. She saw imperfections in her paintings that were invisible to everyone else. While the thought of someone pointing out a flaw sounded kind of absurd to him, he knew it wasn't to her. "I don't think you have anything to worry about, but you couldn't entirely blame someone for wanting to find the coolest part of your work. I bet you've sold a lot more of the kooky ones."

"I haven't sold *a lot* of anything," she said.

"Not yet." She'd only had the pictures up a few weeks. "This might be the next one to go." They'd moved along the wall and stopped in front of a snowy forest at twilight. The sun was low enough in the background that the sky was purplish. The trees were casting long shadows in the snow, except for one. A tree near the center defiantly held its shadow close to its trunk as though not even the sun could tell it what to do. Logan had almost decided it was the one he wanted. She'd done other landscapes where the shadows were too long, too short or going in the wrong direction. This was the only one he'd seen with one different shadow. It seemed symbolic somehow of Audra sharing her work with everyone but him. But mostly he just liked it.

"Is Cameron's job pretty nine to five?" she asked.

"He's a freight forwarder," Logan said, which didn't answer the sudden question. He'd been thrown by a stab of sudden jealousy.

"I know," she said. "I mean, I don't really know much about what he does. I'm just asking if he works regular hours."

"He hasn't mentioned overtime." Logan didn't want to talk about Cameron. Audra had been asking about his birthday last night, too. Why the interest in Cameron? Was it about to happen again? Every time he got his hopes up that his relationship with Audra was about to change for the better, she pulled the rug out from under him. Now he had to wonder if she'd been checking on their Tichu games to see Cameron.

"Do you know what he does in the evenings?" Audra asked. "Like hobbies or standing obligations or anything like that?"

Logan wanted to dissuade her from thinking about Cameron and, fortunately, he had some truth on his side. "I think he's been spending some time talking to a girl."

"A girl?" Her face fell. Perhaps the truth wasn't that fortunate. "You mean he's dating someone?"

"Not exactly. Or maybe not exactly." Logan sighed. "I don't know details. He's tried some online dating that was a disaster, but I don't think he's given up. He's hinted that he's talking to someone who seems promising."

"Do you think you could find out if…" She didn't finish the sentence because Logan was already shaking his head.

There was no way he was getting involved. No way.

She rolled her eyes and said, "Fine."

Logan stepped to the next painting. He needed to get back on topic and get her smiling before he attempted a purchase. "I remember when you brought this one over to show us," he said.

Audra nodded. "Yeah, I did that one pretty recently. Ryan said he liked the way I did the mountains. Then he joked that halftime was over and you guys needed to get back to the game." She frowned at the memory, though she'd laughed at the time. They'd all been complimentary first.

"You should talk to him."

"Ryan?"

"Yes."

"I just saw him last night," Audra said. She didn't sound quite as clueless as she tried.

"I can tell the new job is bothering you," Logan said. "Ryan can probably tell, too. You should talk to him before it gets weird."

She grabbed a section of hair on her shoulder and threw it behind her. "And what am I supposed to say?"

"I don't know. Why does it bother you?"

"It…" Audra turned away and back, twirling her cross pendant between her fingers. She looked as though she wanted to protest but knew it wouldn't be honest.

"Your grandparents talked to you before they offered him the job, didn't they?"

"Exactly," Audra said. "That's why I can't say anything now."

"Why didn't you say anything then?" Logan asked.

"I…" She stood straighter, more defensive. "I wanted to. They just… caught me by surprise."

Logan waited because it appeared she had more to say. There was no need to make her more defensive first.

"I miss working there," Audra continued. "I only quit after high school because I thought I had to. I thought… I don't know, that part of proving I was an adult was proving someone other than family would hire me. Now I do mostly the same stuff at Mackenzie's as I did at the January Café, except it's less fun. I mean, I always took the job seriously. It's just… Mackenzie's is all stuffy and…" She shrugged instead of adding another adjective. "Now I'm wishing I could go back, but Ryan's already quit his job and everything so I'll just…"

"Just get tense and scowl whenever anyone mentions Ryan or the Café or…"

She cut him off with a light punch on the arm, though she also started laughing. "It's not that bad. I know you're exaggerating because I'm really not *that* upset. Plus, I don't scowl."

Logan watched her pretty blue eyes narrow as she dared him to argue. He smiled and kept quiet. He didn't know if he was supposed to point out the scowl or not.

Audra couldn't hold it long before she was also smiling.

It might be now or never. "Obviously, I like all of your paintings," he said, walking back towards the one with the short shadow, "but I think this one is my current favorite. Are you calling it anything?"

"No," she said.

He nodded. Audra didn't officially name any of her work, but now and then one sort of got a nickname like orangey or treeified. "Well, uh, this is the one I want."

Her eyes darted to the painting and back. There was no other indication that she'd even heard him.

"I would like to buy this one," he said. "How much is it?"

"Most people ask how much something is before they announce they want to buy it. Or they don't ask because they've read the sign." She pointed to an easel some distance away.

Logan had read the sign when he came in so he knew, even though it was facing away from him now, that it listed the price of the paintings and the hours Audra was available to sell them. Logan had known both of those things before he came in, too. He'd only asked as an attempt to prompt a transaction. She probably knew that. "Can I buy it now?" he asked.

She shook her head. Her eyes actually scrunched up a little as though she was confused by the idea.

"They are for sale, right?"

"Why do you look surprised?" Audra said. "You know I won't sell you one."

"That was before… when you weren't selling them to anyone."

She shrugged as though that made no difference. But then she took in a big breath. It looked as though she was about to explain something. Her eyes caught sight of something over his shoulder first. "Alison's getting out handles. Come look. It's so cool."

He followed Audra as she dashed over to where Alison was working.

"Can I help?" Audra said.

Alison smiled indulgently. She was sitting on the floor next to a plastic bin of hardware. It looked like a jumble of metal until she started pulling things out. Then Logan could see the separate drawer handles, some of them rubber-banded into sets. "Sure," Alison said.

Audra got on her knees next to her and asked, "What are we looking for?"

"I need two for that." She pointed at an old desk nearby. It had a wide but short drawer across the front. The finish was rough, and it had tiny holes where the handles should be.

Both the women picked through the bin while Logan watched. He could see that Audra was genuinely interested and hadn't deliberately interrupted their conversation. He was happy to see her happy, but he still would've liked to hear why she wouldn't sell him a painting.

"How about these?" Audra held up a pair of glass knobs.

"Those are pretty," Alison said. She took them and set them aside. "But I'm thinking handles might be more practical than knobs. You have to open the drawer with both hands or it gets crooked and stuck. Since it's a desk, someone sitting there might have a pen or something in one hand, and it'd be easier to hook a finger through a handle than grab a knob like that."

Audra nodded seriously. She actually looked just a touch in awe of the wisdom before she resumed her hunt through the bin. After a minute, she held one up for Logan to appreciate. It had an intricate pattern on the metal where it would connect to a drawer. It was mildly interesting, but it did not entice him to join the search.

"Hey," Alison whispered, "you might have a customer." She nodded towards Logan, who was grateful someone remembered his presence until he realized she was nodding past him. An older woman was studying one of Audra's works.

"Oh." She jumped up and smoothed her skirt as she walked over to the woman.

It quickly became apparent they might be talking for a while, and though Alison had put aside a couple of possibilities, she might be looking at handles even longer. Logan felt kind of in the way. "Well, I guess I'll see you later."

Alison looked up and smiled. "Stop by anytime," she said with a wave.

He tried to catch Audra's eye as he left. She waved back with a big smile. It seemed to say he was welcome to come back and buy a painting another time, but he knew that wasn't true. Maybe it didn't mean anything.

3

*A*udra wasn't sure how she was going to break the news. Or when. She'd been putting it off all week and wouldn't have much time between getting home from work and when Alison and Elaine came over for dinner and Tichu.

She tried not to fret too much on the way home and simply enjoyed the feeling of being on the way home. Mackenzie's had always seemed more pretentious than upscale. She had never fit in and felt it more than ever since she'd become wistful for her days at the family restaurant.

When she started at eighteen, her boss had explained that Friday and Saturday nights generally had the best tips and were therefore the most coveted shifts. She was told she might need to work there at least a year to earn that privilege. At the time, Audra had been having a weekly Tichu night with Logan and her brothers so she admitted she actually preferred to have Friday nights off. That had been the wrong thing to say.

Audra had hoped that taking herself out of competition for sought-after shifts might garner favor with new coworkers. Instead, they introduced her to each other as the one who didn't want to work the profitable shifts in a way that made it sound as though she thought she was too good for those shifts. Because she wore a crucifix or cross around her neck, they quickly began joking that she wanted to work as little as possible because she'd taken a vow of poverty. And once that door was open… When she refused dessert, they teased her about thinking sugar was unholy. They stopped talking when she entered the kitchen saying the conversation wasn't meant for pious ears. And today when she agreed to stay an extra hour to cover for someone running late, others joked that she was going to have to go to Confession for working so close to curfew. It was so dumb there was no response.

Audra parked in front of the huge white house where she lived. People called it the Founder's Mansion because it was somehow connected to the town founder, or at least someone in his family. Audra had never really looked into the history. The house was carved into five apartments.

Sometimes Audra would gaze at it before going into her section and imagine she lived in such a big place by herself. She wouldn't know what to do with most of the space, but it was still fun to pretend for a moment. Mostly she imagined she had a separate room for an art studio so she didn't have to spend so much time draping cloths and setting up and cleaning up when she wanted to paint. She shook off the fantasy and work thoughts and went inside.

Violet was in the kitchen staring off into space. "Oh, hi. Uh… we decided on eggs for tonight, right?"

"Yeah, with the cantaloupe," Audra said. "And Elaine's making that crusty bread she was talking about."

"So we won't need the oven."

Audra nodded, though Violet seemed to be talking to herself. They weren't expecting company for nearly an hour. It would be best to say it now, just in case Violet wanted a little time to collect herself. "I need to clean up before dinner and, um, if we end up at the guys' place…"

Violet smirked at her use of the word *if.*

Seeing her happy made it hard to continue, but the situation wasn't hopeless and honesty now might keep Violet from getting her hopes too high. Audra winced internally at the prospect of trying to give some hope but not too much. "Well, I might try to get some more information while we're there about… Logan said he might be seeing someone."

Violet's eyebrows shot up. "Logan is what!?"

"No, Cameron. Logan said *Cameron* might be seeing someone."

"Oh." Violet calmed down. "Might be?"

"Yes," Audra said, glad to hear her roommate focused on the uncertainty. "Logan said he mentioned some sort of online thing but without enough details to know if it was or might be leading to something real."

Violet tipped her head, considering this news. "Cameron's pretty quiet," she said. "I wonder if he's more verbose in print, if he writes her long detailed stories about his day or if he considers complete sentences enough communication."

Audra smiled at the jokey assessment. Something was off though. She certainly hadn't expected Violet to be devastated or anything. But she looked as excited as when they talked about Trevor and Alison getting together. Was there no disappointment at all?

"You'll have to be careful trying to get info," Violet said. "I could see him shutting down if you pushed too hard." She sounded disappointed only at the idea of missing out on details.

"You're right," Audra agreed. Her mind was scrambling to process what this meant. Audra had to have been wrong about which guy had Violet's interest. That was bad. She'd been more upset when she thought Logan was the one becoming unavailable. Violet liked Logan? "I'm going to shower, and then I'll come help you with dinner." Audra caught a nod out of the corner of her eye as she'd already turned towards her room.

Audra shut herself in but did not head towards the bathroom or open a box to find fresh clothes. She stood frozen. Violet liked Logan. Of course she did. Logan was great. He could be as annoying and frustrating as anyone, but he didn't have any serious character flaws. He was honest and loyal. His relationships with God and his family were rock solid. There was plenty to admire about Logan. Plus, there was no denying he was nice to look at.

He had broad shoulders and strong arms that looked like they could wrap you up and keep you safe and… Audra frowned at the direction of her thoughts. She pushed herself towards the bathroom to get ready for the evening. She would enjoy some time with friends, and then she still had a mission. This little surprise didn't change that. In some ways, it actually made the mission easier. Audra knew Logan well. She knew things he would like to do with Violet.

They would be cute together, too. Logan's hair wasn't quite as dark or curly as Violet's. His eyes were light brown, not blue. It wasn't physical features that Audra thought might link them but the overall appearance, their temperaments really. They were both quick with a smile and not easily ruffled. They both enjoyed just hanging out with a friend and a game. Audra considered them her two best friends. She liked them both so much it only made sense they would like each other. If it worked out, she would be happy to see them both happy. Eventually. Surely it would help to know she'd played a part.

After her shower, Audra pulled on a yellow top with a little purple flower on one shoulder. She had to wear plain, all-black clothes to work and usually wanted color afterwards. She ran her hair dryer just long enough that she was no longer dripping. She was picking out a pair of sandals for later when she detected a delicious aroma in the air. Someone was baking something.

Audra returned to the living room and found Violet with a book. "What's in the oven? It doesn't smell like eggs."

"Brownies," Violet said. There was something stiff in her tone, and she hardly glanced up from her book.

Was she worried Audra would be upset? They both tried to keep healthy diets and save desserts for special occasions. They'd agreed when they took the apartment together to help each other by not filling the kitchen with tasty temptations.

It dawned on Audra that the brownies weren't for them. She remembered Cameron saying they didn't need an excuse to bring over a treat. Logan had nodded. Violet made brownies for Logan. But because all the guys agreed, it wouldn't be obvious to him. It would just look like Violet was being thoughtful. She *was* being thoughtful, and Logan would notice. Maybe they wouldn't even need Audra's help getting together.

She grabbed her phone to change the subject with herself. She'd gotten a message while she was in the shower. Ryan wanted to know if he could come over to talk for a minute. Audra hesitated a moment before telling him that was fine. What if he did think she was mad at him? Probably not. Logan didn't know what he was talking about. "Ryan wants to talk about something," she said as she typed out a reply. "He's coming over for a minute."

When Audra looked up, Violet was already gone and her bedroom door shut. It probably wasn't anything that required privacy. But Violet was being thoughtful again.

Since he lived next door, Audra didn't bother sitting down and Ryan knocked before she regretted the choice. "Hi," she said as she let him in.

"Hi." Ryan closed the door behind himself. He stopped before he was fully turned around and inhaled visibly. "What are you guys making over here?"

"Violet's making brownies."

He looked past her, presumably for Violet. He looked back when he didn't see her. "You gonna bring some over to share later?" he asked hopefully.

"Maybe," Audra said. "Maybe we won't save you any."

"Yes, you will."

Audra motioned for him to sit down rather than argue. They both knew she was kidding and that she'd feel worse than he would if she ate a whole pan of brownies just to keep him from having one. She sat on the other end of the couch. "So what's up?"

He glanced around again. "Where's Violet?"

"She's hiding from you."

Ryan actually looked concerned.

"Not really," Audra said. She rolled her eyes at him. How could he know she was kidding one second and not the next? "I told her you wanted to talk about something so she went into her room to give us some space."

"Oh." He nodded, probably at how thoughtful that was.

Audra was having a difficult time not being grumpy about having a thoughtful roommate. Those brownies smelled way too wonderful. She lifted her eyebrows to prompt Ryan to say whatever he came to say.

"Well, today was my last day at Snieders," he said.

Audra nodded. She knew that. She prepared herself to smile when this had to do with how lucky he was to be handed the family business.

"I don't really start at the restaurant until tomorrow, but I've been in there a few times this week, talking to Matt mostly. His wife has a job lined up now as well so it sounds like the move is going to go relatively smoothly for them. In fact, they're talking about leaving a week sooner to stay with her mom until they close on the house." He paused.

Audra hoped he'd gotten most of the way around the giant bush he was beating. "And?" she prompted.

"I think my biggest concern going in will be staffing," Ryan said. "We lost the most reliable daytime server a few months ago, and two more girls are quitting when they start school."

There was an involuntary cringe at his use of the word we. Ryan was already talking as though he was in charge of the place. Audra tried to hide it.

31

"So I was wondering how you might feel about coming back to work there," he said.

Audra blinked. She wasn't sure what she'd been expecting, but that wasn't it.

Ryan talked much faster now that he'd gotten to the point. "You know most of the employees only last a year or two before they move on to something else and most are part time, and I'd feel a lot better if there was someone other than me I could trust to handle training. In fact, I spent most of my time in the kitchen when I worked there so I'm not even sure I'll be able to trust me in the beginning. I know you'd technically be working for me, and working for your brother has the potential to be weird, but I think we could handle it. Plus, we might be able to work something out with your art being next door."

"What do you mean?"

"Well, I don't know exactly," he said. "But maybe Alison could text you if someone's looking at a painting and if things are slow at the restaurant, you could pop over and make a sale without having to make someone come back on Saturday. And regardless, I'd let you have Saturday mornings off so you could keep the arrangement you have there now."

Audra didn't know what to say. She really hadn't sold enough paintings and was unlikely to start selling enough paintings for extra time at Next Love to make a difference. And if she did, it wouldn't be very practical to try to do two jobs at once anyway. But the fact that Ryan was suggesting it, the fact that he was using something she loved to try to convince her to come work for him, that showed it was something he wanted. He wasn't just throwing her a bone in case she felt left out.

"I don't know what you make at Mackenzie's or if we could match it," Ryan said, "but I know we could give you more hours and pay you more than you earned in high school." He stood up. "Now I've made the offer, and you can think about it. Just text me sometime in the next couple of days if you're interested so we can work out all the details."

A timer in the kitchen had started beeping while he was still talking. Audra was glad for the distraction. She wanted to take the job, but part of her still wanted Ryan's job. He saw potential for weirdness without knowing that. Would she be able to keep it to herself if she was working for him?

Halfway to the kitchen, Audra stopped as Violet poked her head out of her room.

"Is it okay if I check on that?" Violet asked.

Audra waved a hand for her to follow. "Please," she said. "Come help me stop the beeping."

Violet dashed ahead and got to the timer first. She switched it off and opened the oven.

"Those smell delicious." Ryan had followed them.

"Thank you," Violet said, carefully setting the hot pan on the stove. Her cheeks were pink from the heat. They probably shouldn't be using the oven in August.

They should be using the stove though. Audra realized with a start that it was nearly six. She shoved Ryan towards the door. "Our real company will be here any minute," she said. "You need to get out so we can get ready."

"Your *real* company?" he repeated, feigning offense. He didn't put up any resistance and moved towards the door with a wave at Violet.

****

Audra looked up and down the street as Ryan disappeared around the building to make sure she wasn't closing the door on Alison and Elaine. No sign of them yet.

Violet was already cracking eggs in the kitchen.

Audra washed her hands and pulled a cutting board from the cupboard.

"What did Ryan want?" Violet asked. "I mean, if it's something you want to tell me."

"He offered me a job."

"Really?" Violet turned, looking fairly surprised.

"Yeah," Audra said. "He said, in so many words, that the turnover at the restaurant worries him, and he'd like to have someone stable out front. I guess it's a compliment."

"You, uh…" Violet rushed her eggshells to the trash, then spoke over the running water. "You don't sound flattered."

Audra sighed. She was trying not to be upset about the whole situation. But even more than that, she was trying not to let everyone know she was upset before she could stop feeling that way. Apparently, Logan wasn't the only one around whom she needed to try harder. "I'm just still surprised," she said.

Violet seemed to accept that answer.

"I'm going to think about it a little more first," Audra said, "but I'm kind of leaning towards saying yes."

"That could be fun," Violet said.

"Fun?"

"Well, fun for a job," she clarified. "You've never liked the atmosphere at Mackenzie's, and your grandparents are cool."

Audra smiled at that truth before she really thought about it. "But they're only there in the morning," she said. "Ryan would probably want me to come in right when they're leaving."

"Uh-oh." Violet turned away from what she was stirring. "Would you have to work Friday nights?"

That was a possible downside to the job. They'd only just established this Friday night routine. Could it survive restructuring? The doorbell rang as the people best able to respond to that question arrived. Audra opened the door for Alison and her mom. She led them to the kitchen among greetings and exclamations of how nice the apartment smelled. The brownies again.

Elaine set the dish she was holding on the counter, then lingered over the aroma of the nearby pan. "I didn't know we were having dessert," she said.

"Well, I didn't, um…" Violet fidgeted a moment before she confessed. "I made it to take to the guys later, but you all have to help me eat some first so it doesn't *look* like I made it just for them."

Elaine nodded knowingly.

"I am happy to help with that," Alison said.

"Maybe you can help Audra, too," Violet said. "With a decision."

The newcomers turned their attention to Audra. "Yeah," she said. "I could use some input, especially regarding how this might affect Friday nights. I love our new game night and don't want to… and it might not because I haven't gotten all the details or even decided for sure about…" She slid into her head for some calculations. Her grandparents, being lifelong morning people, had never established the January Café as a nighttime hangout. It closed at 7 PM most nights. Maybe they would only need to shift the game. Audra refocused on some confused expressions. She paused even longer to be disgusted with herself for being as bad as Ryan about skirting a point.

"She had an interesting visitor just before you got here," Violet said, possibly trying to give Audra a starting place.

"I wouldn't say my brother is particularly interesting," Audra said, "but the visit was. Ryan asked me to come work for him at the restaurant."

"Hmm. Working for family is always a terrible idea," Alison said. She sent her mom a sideways glance before she cracked a smile.

Elaine chuckled at the jab before she addressed Audra. "What do you think about the idea?"

Audra shrugged. "I mostly like it. I'm just concerned that… The restaurant is open until seven on Fridays so if I have to work… it might be 7:30 or later before I can host anyone here."

"I'll be here," Violet said. "We could still have a fixed time and... well, I'd be here even if you were running slightly late."

"That's true," Audra said.

"Do I sound old if I say 7:30 is pretty late for dinner?" Alison asked.

Audra shook her head. She'd been thinking the same thing but didn't want to say anything that might discourage the gathering.

"I could eat whenever," Violet said.

"Well, girls..." Elaine wore the grim expression of someone who hated to be the bearer of bad news but was going to do it anyway. "This might be a good time to mention that I think you should find a fourth from your own generation."

"You don't want to play with us?" Alison asked.

"Do you not like Tichu?" Audra said. She wondered if that had something to do with her not picking it up quickly.

"Oh, no. Don't get me wrong," Elaine said. "I'm having fun, and I'm thrilled that you included an old person like me. But Alison spends so much time with me at the shop. It'd be better for her to have a place she can come to complain about me."

"She has Trevor," Audra pointed out, though she hoped it didn't sound as though she was agreeing that Alison needed to vent about her mom.

"True." Elaine smiled.

Alison blushed.

"But my concentration starts to wane after about 8 o'clock," Elaine continued. "It won't be long before you're all secretly hoping not to be on my team, and I'd rather step aside before that happens." She held up a hand. "I won't abandon you though. I'll stick around until you find a suitable replacement. And if you'll have me, I'd still come watch now and then."

"You'd be welcome," Violet said. "Though if you're willing to stick around until we find a replacement... Well, I don't have any ideas yet."

Audra frowned in concentration. It'd taken her a year to replace what she used to have with Logan and her brothers. It couldn't fall apart so soon. "For now, maybe we could plan on... I mean, if I end up working on Fridays and have to move... Could we plan on skipping only the dinner part? If we ate on our own, we could start the game right away, which might be almost or not much later than we're starting now."

Alison and Violet nodded.

"Sure," Elaine said. "You just work out details with Alison. She's my ride anyway."

"Speaking of starting," Violet said. She picked up the pan of eggs to bring to the table. Somehow, they'd managed to get everything else ready while they were talking. Audra put the cut-up fruit in a bowl then went to wash her hands. Alison took it to the table before she was finished. Elaine remembered where the glasses were, and setting the table had been a group effort. The four women sat down to a nice meal. Audra tried to focus on the moment. Her mind was pulling her forward though, to a new job and what changes it might bring. She felt the peace of knowing this was the direction God was leading her. But God never promised a smooth journey.

4

$\mathcal{L}$ ogan picked up the jack. It had been stuck between his pair of fours so he didn't know he had it until it poked out when he threw the fours on the table.

"I told you the red ones are better," Ryan said.

"That isn't proof of anything but Logan being sloppy," Trevor countered.

Logan tried to focus on what the new jack did to the rest of his hand rather than get drawn into a pointless debate. They had two decks of Tichu cards, one with red backs and one with green. Both decks were old and worn enough that they were a bit sticky and uncooperative. Now and then Trevor and Ryan felt the need to argue about which one was marginally less sticky and uncooperative than the other.

"See how nicely these fan out?" Ryan splayed some red cards from the deck still sitting where Trevor had shoved it aside after the first hand.

Trevor shook his head. "I see several cards clumping together. And I pass."

Ryan also passed. The doorbell rang.

Cameron beat the fours with a pair of fives.

Logan looked up to watch Audra come in as he braced himself to fuel the debate by playing a pair of jacks.

"It's a good thing you found that jack in the sticky cards," Ryan said.

"They're still better than the red ones," Trevor said.

Ryan turned to wave at the women. Violet, Alison and Alison's mom were all right behind Audra. Then he turned back to Trevor. "Was there a pass in that misinformed statement?"

"Yes," Trevor said. "Though I cannot be misinformed about my own *correct* opinion."

"Sounds like trouble in paradise," Audra muttered to her companions. She had already picked up Logan's phone to check the score.

"The red cards are better," Ryan said. "That's not an opinion. It's a fact."

Logan held his hand over the table to see if anyone was going to stop him from taking the trick. Ryan and Cameron quickly passed, and he collected the cards.

"You know, we could avoid all this," Cameron rolled his eyes at Ryan and Trevor, "if you would count your cards to make sure nothing is hiding."

"I trusted you to count them," Logan said, because Cameron had dealt.

He only smiled at the retort. The debate might be pointless, but it was kind of entertaining.

"I always count my cards," Audra said.

Logan tried to glare at her for not being on his side. It was difficult to do when he was happy to see her. She was joining them later now that she had a competing game.

She smiled sweetly, clearly enjoying not being on his side. "Now I'm here, I can count your cards for you," she said. "What'd you do wrong anyway?"

"I didn't do anything," Logan said.

"It's the cards' fault," Ryan said. "These stupid green ones stick together."

"They all stick together." Cameron pointed at Violet. "Just finish the hand so we can break for what they brought us."

Violet was holding a square pan covered with tin foil. Based on an earlier report from Ryan, Logan anticipated brownies. He did not need to be told twice to play faster.

Audra stepped away. She led the women into the kitchen to find plates and was already passing out desserts by the time he had the cards set aside.

Trevor had gotten up. He was enjoying his treat in a corner with Alison where they were probably discussing weekend plans. Violet stood over Trevor's place with a plate in each hand. She set one in front of Ryan and one in front of Logan.

"Thank you," he said.

"Thank you," Ryan echoed. "How are the wedding plans going?"

Violet sighed. "I still don't have a dress."

The brownie had chocolate chips in it. It was rich and moist.

"Still can't agree?" Ryan asked. "Or you just haven't had a chance to look more?"

It was Violet's sister who was getting married. She might have mentioned before that they were having trouble agreeing on her bridesmaid dress. Logan only half-listened. He was trying to focus on savoring the taste but was distracted by Audra hovering behind Ryan. She seemed nervous about something.

Violet shook her head. "She wants me to wear black because she thinks it will look sophisticated. I don't think that's a very happy color for a wedding, but it's her wedding so I'm trying not to argue. But every dress she picks for me is… I just feel like I'm getting ready for a funeral or like a long, boring speech or something."

"You should just agree to whatever she picks out," Audra said, "because you'll look beautiful in anything."

"I'm not trying to be difficult," Violet insisted. "I tried to agree on a couple already, but she could see on my face somehow that I wasn't excited about it and told me we had to keep looking."

Logan became aware that Audra was staring at him expectantly. Not having any idea what she expected, he sort of nodded a little. She seemed appeased but not entirely happy.

"This is so good, by the way," Ryan said. He was down to the last bite of his brownie.

Was that what Audra was looking for? Logan pointed at what was left on his plate. "I said thank you for bringing these over," he repeated, "and I meant it."

Audra wasn't even looking at him anymore. "Uh, Ryan?" she said.

"Yeah." He turned in his chair as she was still mostly behind him.

"I think I like your idea from before." Audra was fiddling with her necklace. "But I wonder if we could talk about it some more later."

"Yes, sure," he said. "You can call me in the morning or… well, I'll be at the restaurant by the time you leave Next Love. You could stop in when you leave."

"Okay," she said.

Something was settled. The way she narrowed her eyes after he turned away suggested it was not her feelings of resentment. Elaine seemed to have continued the dress talk with Violet. She was gesturing to her arm while Violet said something about fabric and texture.

Violet moved to clear the plates as Trevor returned to claim his seat. Alison grabbed her mom, figuratively, and said goodnight to the group as the two of them left. Ryan offered his chair to Violet, then pulled up another one for himself. She scooted back a bit to be out of the way but still have a good view of the game.

Audra had returned to Logan's elbow. He was going to ask if she would also like a chair. Violet probably wouldn't be sticking around if Audra wasn't. She put a hand on his shoulder. "Don't try to get up or do something polite. I'm happy standing and perfectly capable of getting my own chair if I change my mind."

"Okay," he said. "But you don't need to sound like I might hurt myself doing something nice." She didn't need to move her hand either. He liked the feel of Audra leaning on him.

She took her hand away and doubled down as she said, "You might have."

Logan gave the cards another shuffle. Someone usually told him whom to pass them to by now. He thought back to the last hand and realized it was his deal. It took three more rounds to finish the game. They were sort of long but fast at the same time. Audra's presence over his shoulder – she remained standing – made Logan hyperaware, which might have helped his focus except that it was split between her and the combinations in front of him. He and Ryan managed a victory at any rate.

Cameron was the first to say it was time to call it a night, but he was right. They all stood and stretched for a moment before several headed for the door. Cameron looked up long enough to wave but had his phone in his hand and was somewhat absorbed as he walked to his car. They came out the side of the big house. Violet said goodnight and skipped around the front without waiting for Audra, who seemed to be dragging her feet.

Was she looking for a chance to talk to Logan alone? That was an opportunity he would gladly seize. "Are you and Ryan working things out?" he asked.

She faced him abruptly and said, "I'm not mad at him."

"I know," he agreed reflexively. She sounded a bit mad though. It was probably because he brought it up. "I... um... you said something about talking to him tomorrow. It seemed significant."

She folded her arms and leaned against the side of the house. "He asked me to work for him. *For* him, even though I'm the one with more experience."

Logan nodded that he was listening without saying anything. It was true that Audra had worked at the January Café longer and more recently. But Ryan had five years more work experience in general. He'd been involved with the hiring at his last job, and he had a four-year degree that Audra did not. If it wasn't a family business, it'd be obvious who was more qualified to manage the place. It was a family business though. Logan kept his mouth shut and simply tried to appear sympathetic. It wasn't an act. He hated that she was upset.

"I know he's older," Audra said. "But…" She stopped talking and let her eyes communicate the rest of the thought.

Logan got that she wasn't convinced age was an adequate consideration. If he was supposed to interpret anything else, they were both out of luck. He wouldn't mind trying for a while though. Her eyes were like magnets to his, soft but irresistible magnets. He might have even taken a step closer before he realized she was waiting for a response.

"Are you going to work for him?" he asked.

"I think so." Audra pushed herself away from the house and farther from Logan in the process. "As soon as I started thinking about leaving Mackenzie's, I started realizing how much I want to. So I hope I'm not letting one bad situation push me into another."

Logan did not like the sound of that. "You really think it would be *bad* to work for Ryan? I don't think he'd micromanage or anything. He'd respect that you know what you're doing."

"I know," Audra said, and she even smiled faintly. "Because I'm really not mad at him. I'm just kind of mad at me and wish I had time to process that before… but I don't want to miss this chance to do what I'm kicking myself for not doing before."

"So you won't be kicking Ryan?" Logan teased.

"No."

"And you're not… Are you bottling up some feelings to kick him with later?"

"No," she said. "I'm not trying to bottle up or bury anything. I'm just… Mature people are in control of their feelings and not the other way around. I guess I'm just not mature enough to snap my fingers and stop pouting. Not that I'm pouting." She threw him a dirty look as though he was the one who had suggested it.

"You're not going to kick me, are you?"

She laughed and said, "Don't tempt me." Then she sobered. "It actually helps to say it out loud and know this conversation won't come back to haunt me. You're not going to tell Ryan or Grandma May that I'm bubbling with resentment just to cause trouble, are you, Bartholomew?"

He loved hearing her use his first name. She hadn't done that in a long time, and her tone still made it sound like an intimate secret. "I do like to cause trouble but not that kind."

"You're right about the other kind." Audra grinned at him. "My mom still talks about the time you talked Trevor into forking the neighbor's lawn."

"I think if you check the record on who talked who into what, you'll see that you have your facts wrong. Plus, they started it."

Audra laughed. "That whole thing was… Even when my mom tries to sound disapproving, you can tell she thought it was funny. Except for the mailbox thing."

"Well, that was why we had to go nuclear with the forks. It didn't do any real damage, but we knew Mr. Ruff would step in if we messed with his lawn."

"The funniest part," Audra said, "was how Ryan took your share of the blame. He was away at school and physically could not have been involved and yet… Mom said Mr. Ruff mentioned it recently, just kidding around now that it's in the past but still joked about how he hoped her boys were behaving themselves."

"Yeah, I don't know," Logan said. "Maybe I was at your house so much people thought I *was* Ryan."

"Because you guys look so much alike?"

The sarcasm was nice because Logan wanted to believe she saw him much differently than she saw her brothers. Or at least that she might someday soon.

She sighed at the memory.

Logan didn't want to leave, but leaving on a high note was probably the best he could hope for. "I guess I should head home."

"Um…" Audra moved slightly into his path. "Before you go… can I ask you a favor?"

He nodded.

"Well…" She studied the sidewalk and looked as though she was trying to think of a favor.

He didn't know what she was thinking. That wasn't really anything new, although trying to conjure a request was. As the silence stretched, Logan felt a growing desire to take her hands, pull her close, and assure her he'd do anything. But then he was hit by a disturbing idea. What if she was trying to word a favor that had to do with interest in Cameron? Even a clumsy redirect would be better than that. "If you're going to ask me to buy a painting," he said, "the answer is yes."

Audra looked up and bore her gaze into his. "Why do you keep joking about that?"

"I'm not joking," he said. "I honestly would like one of your paintings. Sell it to me. Give it to me. I don't care."

"That's why," she said.

He closed his eyes. Maybe she was trying to drive him crazy. "I don't understand."

She put her hands on her hips, tilted her head, then slowly began to shake it rather than explain anything. "Can I ask the real favor now?"

"Have you decided what it is?"

"Yes." She motioned towards her front door. "Will you come over for dinner tomorrow night?"

Spending time with her was a favor? He didn't need to think about that one. "Okay," he said.

"Um... 6 o'clock?"

"That'll work."

"Okay. Great. Goodbye." She blew out what seemed like nervous energy. "See you tomorrow."

She rushed to get inside, leaving Logan to walk to his car as confused as ever. He gripped the steering wheel tighter than necessary but took one hand off to wave when he noticed Audra looking out the window. Why was she watching out the window after saying goodbye in a hurry? Why did she do anything?

She'd flat out told him there would never be anything beyond friendship between them so he shouldn't have any reason to hope. But she kept silently contradicting herself. She seemed to find excuses to hang around. Every Friday, she stood closer to Logan than either of her brothers. She never tried to look at Cameron's cards. She'd recently invited Logan to lunch. It turned out to be part of a ploy to get Trevor and Alison together. Still, he'd been the one she thought of to help. He was the one she was talking to about what was bothering her. And now dinner. Logan knew it wasn't a romantic overture, but he could sense something in her demeanor that suggested she wanted it to be. Or maybe he was already crazy.

5

*A*lison's dad was in her work space when Audra arrived. Audra hadn't seen much of him yet because he preferred to spend time in the back room with the furniture that didn't expect small talk. But there were no customers in the shop at the moment.

Audra waved at Elaine, who was dusting pieces by the opposite wall.

"Good morning, Audra," she called. She set down her rag and exchanged it for a white coffee mug, apparently intent on following.

"Morning, Alison," Audra said. "Morning, Mr. Brachy. Nice to see you out and about."

He nodded seriously. "I like to watch my girl at work now and then. Makes a man proud to see his skills passed on."

Alison rolled her eyes. "Nice speech, Dad. But that's not the real reason you're out here." She turned to Audra. "Mom just got a text from Sheila that she's on her way."

"I assure you I'm not out here to talk to that woman," he said.

"Yeah, you just want her to see you run into the back," Alison said.

Her dad folded his arms across a broad chest. He was probably around sixty but had the physique of a man accustomed to an active life. The stance made him look like someone no one wanted to mess with. "I do not run away from her," he said.

"She enjoys the act anyway," Elaine said.

A grunt was the only response.

Alison dipped her brush into a can of stain or varnish or something for the wood. Audra didn't have the skills to properly name it. Watching was somewhat fascinating while she felt the anticipation of Sheila's arrival. Audra hadn't met Sheila yet, though she was predisposed to like her. It was when she found out the Brachys sold jewelry on Sheila's behalf that Audra got the idea to approach them about her paintings.

The anticipation hung in the air only a few moments before the door opened. Alison glanced up and mouthed, "That's her," as her mom moved towards the front.

The woman who entered appeared close to Elaine's age. She wore a dress with a bold flowery print. Her necklace of black beads had several strands and her chin-length hair was dyed a deep black. She charged towards the back of the shop. The briefcase she carried clattered loudly when she dropped it on a table near her jewelry case and kept walking. Elaine met her partway and turned to accompany her while offering pleasantries, though Sheila didn't smile.

The newcomer stopped only when she was close enough to pin her eyes on Alison. "I hear you've taken up with a man."

Audra felt her eyes widen at this accusation. Jim Brachy was already striding towards the door to the back room. Alison's only reaction was a small nod of confirmation.

"What's his name?" Sheila demanded.

Alison glanced at her mom, then said, "Trevor Norman."

"Hmm. Norman? Why does that name sound familiar?" She drilled her gaze into Elaine.

"May Norman runs the place next door," Elaine said with a wave that direction. "He's her grandson."

"May's all right," Sheila said. "I don't know what she was thinking having sons or grandsons though. Must've been Paul's idea."

Audra felt herself relax somewhat. As gruff as this woman was, the nonsense in her words softened the situation.

Alison's dad returned holding a styrofoam cup with steam rising from the top. He handed it to Sheila before he disappeared again. She held it under her nose for a moment, then lowered it without taking a sip. "I suppose you like this guy?"

"So far," Alison said. "We have only been dating a few weeks."

"Ah." Sheila nodded. "So you have time to come to your senses?"

Alison shrugged. Her lips twitched against a smile that said she didn't want to come to her senses.

Sheila seemed to understand that because she frowned disapprovingly.

"Did you bring some new inventory today?" Elaine asked.

Sheila was still fixed on Alison. "You do know that a man will not improve your life, right?"

There was a pause while Alison considered her response. She answered with a serious tone. "Maybe I can improve his."

Sheila almost smiled. For just a moment, she looked impressed despite herself. She schooled her features before turning back to Elaine. "I do have items to restock. But first I'd like to meet the new artist. This her?" She jabbed her thumb towards Audra.

"Yes." Elaine cleared her throat and adopted a formal attitude. "Where are my manners? Sheila Bierly, this is Audra Norman."

Sheila had begun to extend a hand to Audra when she froze. "Norman? Are you somehow responsible for Alison's unfortunate condition?"

"Uh…" Audra had to suppress a laugh before she could answer, which gave her a moment to decide how to answer. She was proud of her small role in getting Trevor and Alison together, but this did not feel like a time to brag. "Trevor is my brother," she said.

"I suppose you can't help that." She finished the handshake, then nodded towards the art on the wall. "And I'm impressed with what I can see from here. Do you mind if I take a closer look?"

"Definitely not," Audra said. She followed Sheila to her nearest painting, then held her breath while she waited for a reaction.

Sheila studied it for a few seconds before she pointed at a stream in the foreground. "Got that one," she said as she moved to the side. "The clouds."

"Good eye," Elaine said. She had come along as well and leaned in a bit. "I already told Sheila about the kooky parts of your work and how it takes me a while to spot them. She's trying to show me up."

"I am not," Sheila said. "You just made it sound like a game to hunt them. This one is…" She was talking with her eyes glued to a picture. She turned her head to the side as her words trailed off, then she stepped back as she turned to Audra. "It's like the cave is floating. It's gotta be either brilliant or insane, and you're making whatever it is work for you."

"Thank you," Audra said, though she wasn't entirely sure it had been a compliment.

"Duty calls." Elaine slipped away as a customer entered the store.

Sheila sipped at her coffee, staring at the same painting. Her eyes flicked briefly to Audra. "I'd like to ask how bad it is, but I suppose you're biased."

"What?" Audra didn't quite feel offended, more prepared to be offended as soon as she understood the question.

"He's a man," Sheila said. She lifted her cup the direction they'd left Alison. "But I hope your brother is at least better than most."

"Oh, you mean Trevor." Audra was momentarily relieved that her work was not being criticized. But this woman she'd just met had no right to malign her family either. "Trevor is… I can tell you he would never intentionally hurt anyone."

"Hmm." The frown lines on her face didn't soften. "Well, I

could look at this art for some time, but I have quite a to do list for today. I need to drop off my merchandise and talk business with Elaine."

Audra watched her return to her briefcase. Sheila set her now half-empty cup on a table and snapped open the case. She pulled out several colorful necklaces – they sparkled even from a distance – and hung them in the armoire. She removed a few items to take with her as well.

Once the briefcase was back in her hand, she marched over to Elaine and clearly interrupted the conversation with a customer. Alison had apparently been ready for that. She'd left her work area while Sheila was swapping out her jewelry and was close enough to jump in to discuss the dresser that had caught someone's interest.

The scene left Audra somewhat disillusioned. She had heard there was animosity between Sheila and Alison's dad. But she'd pictured something more playful, more like when she was teased by her brothers. Audra had also been excited to meet Sheila and share the bond of selling creative items in the midst of functionality. It was going to be hard to like Sheila.

A few other customers came in around the time Sheila left. None of them showed much interest in Audra's paintings, but she was asked a few questions about the furniture. She'd been paying enough attention that she was somewhat helpful, though she made a point of clarifying that she didn't actually work there. Shortly before she was scheduled to leave, she found a few quiet minutes to talk to Alison, who was still trying to finish staining the piece she'd been working on all morning.

Audra plopped herself onto a chair. "Okay, what's the deal with Sheila?"

"The deal?" Alison nodded knowingly. "I tried to warn you she's a, uh, strong personality."

"You didn't tell me she's a man-hater."

"It doesn't always come up," Alison said. "I should have predicted she'd have something to say about me dating someone."

"Something to say about it?" Audra scoffed. "I'm surprised she didn't ask for his address so she could go hunt him down."

Alison laughed. "She's definitely a bark is worse than the bite sort of person."

"The bark is bad enough."

"Yeah." Alison put down her brush. "Do you really want to know the story?"

"So there is a story?"

"Sheila and my mom have been friends since they were kids," Alison began. "They lived near each other. Sheila is a year older, which means she was in my dad's class actually. She graduated a year before my mom. She got married that summer to a guy that I guess her parents didn't like." Alison exhaled sadly. "The marriage only lasted about three months. He was apparently really cold about it, just told her one day that he'd realized being married was like being caught in a beartrap and that she needed to leave before he wanted to chew his leg off."

Audra's mouth fell open. She could understand Sheila's attitude towards a particular man. "He said that?"

Alison nodded.

"And he made *her* leave?"

"Yeah, it was bad. She had moved from her parents' house to his apartment, and she didn't have a job because she had hoped she was going to have their first kid right away and… Anyway, she was too humiliated to tell her parents that maybe they'd been right not to like the guy, and she spent a few nights in a homeless shelter before my mom told her parents. They invited her to stay with them until she could get on her feet."

"Wow." Audra absorbed and processed the story. Though it didn't make Sheila any more likable, it did make her more sympathetic. "I'm really sorry she got treated like that. It's awful.

But being bitter this long has got to be hurting her more than anyone else. I mean, it's been like forty years, right?"

Alison bit her lip while she figured some mental math. "At least," she said. "My mom says she doesn't really hate all men, that once she realized there are some wonderful men in the world, she actually hurt worse because she had to blame herself for choosing poorly. But she also says Sheila's not as bitter as she sounds, that she got some bad habits before she healed."

"I suppose rudeness is as much a bad habit as a personality trait."

"True." Alison dropped her brush in a can of cleaner and stood up to stretch her legs. "Though the general attitude does make it easier to ignore comments about my dad. And now Trevor."

Audra nodded. Sheila's disapproval of Trevor would have been more insulting if she had based it on anything personal.

They'd been talking with low voices as more customers began to browse. Alison tipped her head towards the main part of the shop and said, "I better... mingle."

"Of course." Audra stepped back to let Alison do her job and to position herself closer to her paintings in case any of the customers could become her customers. A few people asked questions or offered compliments. No one bought a painting though. That was disappointing, possibly more so because of the stress involved. Audra hoped she'd eventually get used to having her work on display, but it hadn't happened yet. She was emotionally invested in each of those paintings and felt raw and exposed with them out where anyone could walk up and judge them.

It was something of a relief when it was time to go next door to the familiar family restaurant. At noon, it was about half full. They did more lunch business during the week than on Saturdays. Audra took a seat at the end of the counter at the back rather than sit at a table by herself.

"Hello. What can I... oh. You're, like, family, right?" This greeting was delivered in monotone by a teenage boy wearing an apron and holding a notepad.

Audra nodded because she understood what he was asking. No one in the family got charged for meals at the January Café. Audra thought this was a nice perk when her grandparents offered it, but that it was embarrassing when employees carried it out. She was afraid they would think she thought it made her someone important. "I'm actually not here to eat," she said.

Then she stopped herself before she waved him away. It occurred to her that Ryan might not have a chance to talk to her right away. And she was hungry. It wouldn't hurt to have something to munch on. She ordered a simple lunch and sat back to wonder whether it would arrive before or after her brother.

She didn't see Ryan so he must have been in the kitchen. Scanning the room, she did see a few people she recognized. Some because they were regular customers and some from other places around town. Her eyes kept returning to a young woman she didn't know who was sitting alone in a corner. There was a book open in front of her.

Audra had first noticed her right as the door opened. The woman's eyes had jumped up at the sound. It appeared she was expecting someone. Maybe a date? Audra's romantic sensibility hoped it was a date. The next time the door opened, she turned to it as well wanting to see a young man with flowers. It was a bunch of guys in dirty boots and reflective vests. The woman had returned her attention to her book.

"Hey, sis." Ryan was now standing on the other side of the counter, leaning on it with both hands. "What do you need to know before you agree to help me out?"

She smiled as she thought that he should remember who was helping whom when they were working together. They talked mostly about the schedule, about how Saturday mornings at Next Love would be enough, and a bit about changes in procedures since she last worked there. It was agreed that they would pick a start date as soon as she knew her last day at Mackenzie's.

Audra's food had arrived while they talked so she stayed to finish after Ryan returned to the kitchen. She had ordered a salad and someone forgot to put the dressing on the side. Ryan hadn't noticed until after the server left. He offered to fix it, but Audra insisted it would be fine. She didn't want it to go to waste or make the boy who messed up feel like he was in trouble. She sat awhile pushing the most soaked leaves around to hunt edible bites.

That other young woman was there almost as long. She had continued to watch the door but was never joined by anyone. Audra sensed that she was both disappointed and relieved when she left. Was it a blind date perhaps? That would explain why she might have been excited but also nervous enough to be relieved the guy didn't show up.

Of course, it could also be explained by Audra's imagination. She might have been projecting her own mixed feelings about dinner. Was it a mistake to invite Logan? Audra could see that Violet was a little envious of her sister getting married. She wanted to see Violet paired up with a nice guy, wanted to help even. But why did it have to be Logan? As much as Audra wanted her matchmaking scheme to work out, she couldn't honestly say she'd be disappointed if it didn't. She slipped a tip next to her plate and left the restaurant to go home and plan for the evening.

6

ogan shut off the engine and glanced at the big Founder's
Mansion. He wasn't there to play cards with the guys.
He was going to Audra's door because she had asked him. Hope that
things were finally going to work out with her just would not go away.
He closed his eyes and prayed that she would give him some sort of
signal on what to do here. The prayer included a plea that she would
use words with the signal, simple ones.

Logan resisted the urge to run up the sidewalk and stifled the
wince when Violet answered the door. "Hi, Violet," he said.

"Hi, Logan." She stepped back. "Come on in."

They joined Audra in the kitchen where three plates had
already been set at the table.

He peered over her shoulder into a pan. "Chicken?"

She nodded and pointed to a big pot with a lid. "We also have
some broccoli and cauliflower steaming."

"Sounds good," he said. At least there was meat. Sometimes
Audra liked to eat meals that were about as filling as air. He'd seen
her put a touch of whipped cream on a pile of fruit and call it dessert.
"Did you talk everything out with Ryan this afternoon?"

"Yep." Audra turned away from the stove to face Logan and
Violet, who stayed on the other side of the table. "I'll tell Bonnie
that I'm quitting tomorrow and whatever she wants to be my last day,
I'll probably go back to the good restaurant the next one."

Violet nodded as though she'd already heard that plan.

Logan decided not to press for more information and simply hope that she and Ryan would be able to work together.

"Do you need me for anything else?" Violet asked. Her eyes darted to the side as though she might have something to do in another room.

"Oh, no," Audra said. "We're ready to eat." She picked up the pan with the chicken and carried it to the table. Then she looked at Logan and pointed to a chair.

He happily complied with the nice, clear instruction.

Violet brought over the vegetables. The two women conferred behind Logan for a minute before they placed a few more things on the table. Violet ended up sitting next to him and Audra facing him. The three of them bowed their heads to thank God for the food, then began to pass it around.

Audra smirked as she started the conversation. "I think I found a new nickname for Trevor today."

Violet laughed.

Logan said, "What is it?"

"You know I was at Next Love this morning," she said, "and I met Sheila. She's the woman who makes the jewelry." She paused to see if he was following and to add a little anticipation.

"Okay," Logan prompted.

"The woman is not a fan of anyone with a Y chromosome and wasn't happy to hear that Alison had gotten involved with one." Audra smiled at her impending reveal. "She referred to Trevor as Alison's unfortunate condition."

Violet seemed to enjoy the story.

Logan smiled only because Audra enjoyed it and because he knew that was a nickname that would never catch on. It was way too long. He added a few shakes of salt to his veggies.

"I'm sorry if it's bland," Audra said. "Everything at Mackenzie's is drenched in sauce or crusted with seasoning and sometimes I just want to taste my food and not a symphony of flavor or whatever."

"It isn't… Okay, it *is* bland, but that's not your fault," Logan said. "It's cauliflower's fault. I mean, it even looks bland."

Audra seemed to think his opinion of cauliflower was funny so he hadn't offended her by adding salt, which should not have been on the table if it was a trap.

"Well, I agree with Audra," Violet said. "A little bit of seasoning can enhance the flavor, too much just covers it up. I put in a bit of salt while it was cooking."

Audra put her hand near her mouth to share an aside with Violet. "Now he's thinking that cauliflower has no flavor to cover up."

That was exactly what he'd been thinking so he went ahead and added more salt. Both the women laughed and rolled their eyes in response.

"The chicken is good," Logan said, just in case anyone was not as amused as she looked.

"So I guess my new work schedule has some bad news for Violet, and some more bad news."

"It's not going to be a problem," Violet said.

Logan looked between them to see who was going to explain.

"You know right now I take over our living room with my paint whichever weekday I have off," Audra said. "Violet's at work so it doesn't bother her. The January Café is closed on Sundays so I think I'm going to have to make that my new painting day."

Violet chewed faster to be able to answer. "I'm sure I can stay out of your way."

"I'm worried about staying out of *your* way," Audra said.

Violet just shook her head. She seemed sincere that she wouldn't mind.

A mischievous glint flashed in Audra's eyes. "Of course, if my efforts to get you an unfortunate condition of your own pays off, you might have someone to keep you busy."

It took Logan a moment to remember the nickname from earlier but much less time to decide he wanted to steer clear of that topic, especially with Violet's eyes shooting daggers at Audra. Though he silently noted that another guy at the table might balance things out. "What was the other bad news?" he asked.

"Huh?" Audra wrinkled her eyes. "Oh, right. I said more bad news. That's worse. I'll have to work Fridays. Ryan said he'd get me out as close to seven as possible, but that'll still push our new Tichu game back. Elaine already said she doesn't want to stay so late, and I'm afraid the weekly game is going to fall apart if I can't find a replacement."

"Could you do it a different night?" Logan asked.

"I don't think so." Audra let out a defeated sigh. "I'd have the same problem every weekday, and Violet sees her parents Sunday nights so it'd have to be Saturday."

"If it was Saturday, I could be your fourth." Logan thought that was a great idea. He'd see her twice a week.

Audra was already shaking her head.

"You're not a girl," Violet said.

"Yeah, it's a girls' thing now," Audra said. "And I just feel like more things would get in the way on Saturday. Besides, Friday is Tichu night."

It was difficult to argue with that statement. Friday had been Tichu night for years. Logan regretted the way Audra had been pushed out to make room for Cameron – not that anyone asked his opinion at the time – so he understood her desire to exclude guys in response. Having two games was a good solution. "Alyssa knows how to play," he said, "but her bedtime is probably more strict than Elaine's."

Audra had brightened before he got to the end of the sentence, then frowned at him for suggesting a wrong answer.

"How old is she?" Violet asked.

"Twelve."

"Hmm." She frowned as well. "So if we still need someone in a few years…"

Logan wasn't helping. He was kind of disappointed in himself for the idea. He wanted to help and had started talking before he thought it through.

"We have time to figure it out or convince Elaine to stick around," Audra said.

"She did promise not to abandon us," Violet added.

"We'll be resourceful somehow." Audra shared a desperate but hopeful look with Violet before she met Logan's eyes. "You know, asking Alyssa probably would have made Jack jealous anyway."

Another reason his idea was bad. He was so glad she pointed that out.

"What have you been doing with those two lately?" Audra asked.

"Bowling."

Audra nodded as though she awaited him to elaborate on the answer.

Logan had two much younger siblings. Jack was only two years older than Alyssa. He usually took the two of them out somewhere on Sunday afternoons to give their parents the house to themselves for a little while. "I took them about a month ago and Alyssa beat Jack. He wanted a rematch, which he also lost. He did win once, but they both want to go every week now. It's gotten fairly competitive."

"Do you play, too?" Violet asked.

"Yeah. Neither of them has beaten me yet."

"Of course." Audra's tone suggested he hadn't needed to mention that.

But Logan had been talking about who was winning the games. It was an important detail.

"Hey! I just thought of something." Audra pointed at Violet. "Violet has never been bowling."

"Never?" He turned to Violet.

She shrugged. "My mom said I was invited to a bowling birthday party sometime in elementary school, but I got sick and couldn't go. I guess I missed my chance."

"Not necessarily." Audra pointed at Logan, then Violet. "You should take her next week. Not with Jack and Alyssa, but... um, on Saturday afternoon. It's perfect. Violet can have a new experience, and you can get some extra practice so you don't get beaten by a twelve-year-old."

Violet snorted at the joke.

"I don't need extra practice," Logan said. He circled his hand around the table. "All three of us could go though."

"No, um... no," Audra said. "Just you two." Her eyes were boring into Logan while her head tipped to the side, indicating he was supposed to say or do something.

He turned slowly to Violet. "Do you want to give it a try?"

She looked at Audra for an answer, whom he caught giving her a small but vigorous nod.

"Okay," Violet said.

"Great. I'll look forward to hearing about it." Audra leaned towards Violet. "If you crack a hundred, you will have beaten my record."

Audra was a terrible bowler. That was probably why she wanted to sit this one out. And it sounded as though Logan could still see her afterwards. "So I should come by to get you around..." He was talking to Violet, but neither of them was surprised when Audra answered.

"2 o'clock?"

At least she seemed to be checking if the time would work for them.

When she got nods, she said, "Perfect."

Logan helped himself to another piece of chicken, then asked Audra what she planned to paint next. She had a few ideas but hadn't settled on anything. Violet had some suggestions, which Audra appeared to consider. Logan was sure any of them would look wonderful in Audra's skilled hands. He carefully avoided saying anything about how much he'd like to have one. They were getting along too well.

Violet had a funny story from work – she was a receptionist and occasionally answered odd calls – that got everyone laughing. The three of them sat talking long after the food was finished. He stayed to help clean up but then decided he shouldn't overstay. He thanked them for the meal and saw himself out.

****

The moment the door closed behind Logan, Violet turned wide eyes on Audra. "Your new mission is moving forward already, huh?"

Audra nodded, but she was concerned by Violet's trepidation. "You said it was okay if I got involved. Is it still okay?"

"Yeah. Uh… sure. I just didn't expect you to come up with a plan so quickly."

"I'm good," Audra said. She didn't feel good though. Deep down, she felt a little sick. She took a seat on the couch and hugged a pillow to her stomach to cover it.

Violet sat on the other end with one leg tucked under her to face Audra. "Here's what I think," she said. "If you're going to get involved with my love life, it's only fair that you finally fill me in on yours." She pointed to the door Logan had exited. "What's the history there?"

Audra pinched her lips together while she thought about how to answer. They had never really talked about Logan. Violet had always respected her privacy where he was concerned, but she had a good point that the situation had changed, or was about to change.

62

Her relationship with Violet would get messy fast if she revealed how much she cared about Logan or if Violet imagined something on his side that wasn't there. Perhaps being honest about as much of the history as she could was the best way to move forward.

"You admitted once that you had a crush on him in high school," Violet said patiently. "I've always kind of expected… but nothing seems to be happening."

"Nothing is going, um…" Audra paused to focus her mind on the past. "Logan and I have been friends for almost as long as he's been friends with Trevor and Ryan. But, yes, I did start fantasizing that he was the one I was going to someday marry when I was like fifteen or sixteen."

Violet nodded. That was the part she knew.

"My parents had talked to me about trying to avoid any romantic relationships while I was still in high school," Audra continued. "They didn't tell me I couldn't date, but they encouraged me to do it in groups and avoid official labels that might be hard to… unlabel. And I actually had a friend who called this one guy her boyfriend immediately and then after they'd gone out a few times she decided she didn't really like him and didn't know how to break up with him and it got seriously bad because it ended up like everyone else knew she didn't like him anymore before he did and… enough tangent."

Violet laughed.

"So Logan knew all that. The part about my parents, not… Well, they had had similar conversations with Ryan and Trevor. It wasn't a girl thing. I kind of thought that he liked me, too, but knew as well as I did that it would be tricky to keep things slow when he was at my house all the time. I mean, it would be hard to get to know each other without really dating when we already knew each other so I guessed he was just waiting for me to finish high school. At least that was my take on the situation. But I guess I wanted proof."

"Proof?" Violet sounded confused, but she still leaned forward because she sensed this was where the story was going to get interesting.

"There was this guy in my chemistry class, my lab partner actually. We talked some between steps and stuff. He asked me out, and I didn't like him like that at all. I thought it would be better to tell him I wasn't allowed to date. He wanted to do something just the two of us, which I sort of wasn't... Anyway, he said okay. But he asked again a few days later and tried to convince me that it wouldn't be that hard to get together without my parents finding out. He even teased me about being a baby for following their rules, which of course was a big turnoff so I just flat out told him no at that point. We only talked about chemistry stuff after that."

"Okay, nice story," Violet said. She was smiling enough to appear appreciative. "But I'm not connecting the dots. What does chemistry guy have to do with Logan?"

"Well..." Audra hesitated as the more interesting part was also the more embarrassing part. Then she plunged back into the story, reminding herself that she had matured considerably in the intervening years. "I decided to tell Logan about the situation that wasn't really a situation to see if he sounded jealous. I know, it was stupid. But I got Logan alone and told him how the guy wanted me to lie to my parents because he wanted to spend time with me so badly, and I asked what he thought of that. He said that no guy who respected me and cared about me would ask me to sacrifice my principles for him."

"Nice." Violet nodded with approval. "Did he sound jealous though?"

"Not really, but I still felt I got my answer. I was sure he was hinting that *he* cared enough to wait. And there was something about the phrasing of sacrificing my principles that made me feel important in his eyes, like someone with principles, which... I mean, of course I had principles. That's..." Audra shook her head against how little sense those thoughts now made. "Anyway," she said, "let's just say I inflated the conversation into some sort of intimate contract in my head. Then he almost kissed me."

Violet sat back and squealed. "Slow down! I need details on the almost and you gotta explain how that was bad because you said it like it totally sealed the fate of you *not* getting together. Was that part of the same conversation?"

"No, it was later." She had skipped ahead on purpose to see Violet's reaction. It was worth it. "A few months after we talked about chemistry guy, we were all playing Tichu, me and Logan and Ryan and Trevor. Both of my brothers left the table for a minute. I think Trevor brought laundry home from school, and he was working on that or... I don't remember what Ryan was doing."

"It doesn't matter," Violet said.

Audra smiled at her eagerness. "So Logan and I were sitting next to each other, alone, and it was my deal but he had half the cards. He put his hand out for my half and said he would shuffle for me, and I told him I was perfectly capable of shuffling myself. I pushed his hand away with one of mine and reached over to take the cards from him with the other. But I didn't want to bend or damage the cards so I wasn't very forceful. I was just trying to gently pry his fingers open, and I kind of realized I was still touching his other hand, too. The mood suddenly got more serious, and I could tell he was getting closer and... I don't know. We just both kind of pulled back at the same time. I was sitting there all self-conscious like what just happened? Logan shoved the cards towards me without saying anything. Then just before Trevor came back, he said, 'You don't have to tell anyone about that.'

"I couldn't believe he was asking me to be secretive after I'd built him up as this paragon of virtue who respected all my principles and stuff. I got mad. He seemed to know that I was mad but not *why*, and that made me more mad and things just got weird. We were kind of avoiding each other, then we didn't see as much of each other when I went to college. By the time I dropped out and came home, I was less swoony around him, and it was clear he wasn't interested in me as more than a friend." Audra stopped, wincing inside at leaving out the part that made that clear. But it was too recent. Violet would never believe her romantic interest had completely disappeared.

Violet seemed to be mulling over the details. "Are you sure that... I still think he likes you."

"As a friend and maybe even like a sister. That's all," Audra said. "Now... moving on... My plan will work. Don't worry."

"All right. Thanks for sharing as much as you did." Violet glanced around. "Do you think I have time to do laundry before bed?"

7

The week had been a whirlwind of change. Audra slipped a black apron over her head and reached behind her back to tie it. She didn't mind this black when she could wear whatever she wanted with it. And the January Café logo was scribbled across the front in a friendly font. Though she couldn't explain how a font was friendly.

Audra had told her boss on Monday that she wanted to put in notice. Bonnie had replied that since she never really wanted to be there anyway, they might as well call Monday her last day. She kind of felt as though she'd been fired for quitting. And it wasn't fair to say she never wanted to be there only because she never vied for the coveted shifts. The end result was the same so she tried not to dwell on it. When she told Ryan, he invited her to start on Tuesday. The next few days had been a strange mix of new and nostalgia.

In the four years since she'd worked there, the restaurant itself hadn't changed much. The chairs along the counter still had red stripes. The coffee mugs were on the same shelf behind it. Everything in the kitchen seemed as she remembered it, right down to the creepy shadow by the cooler that had once given her nightmares. But even though it looked the same, it felt different. It was a real job now, not helping her grandparents for a few hours a week.

Grandma May and Grandpa Paul were retired, or at least called themselves retired. They still came in to open the place at 6 o'clock every morning and stayed until 10 o'clock, which was the start of Audra's shift. She arrived a few minutes early to chat or they stayed a few minutes. The middle of the morning was generally pretty quiet.

Ryan didn't seem to want to take advantage of the chance to start out slowly. He went straight to the kitchen to look over the schedule and count boxes and make sure none of the supplies had escaped overnight. Audra left him to it as she went back out front.

"Have a good day, Audra," called a gruff male voice.

She waved to John, who was on his way out the front door.

There were four old guys, friends of her grandpa, who came in for breakfast every morning. Grandpa Paul sat with them whenever he wasn't needed elsewhere. Two of the guys were less retired than the others and left when it was still somewhat early. The other two hung around until Grandpa was getting ready to leave. Audra moved towards their table in the corner. Grandpa Paul had stood up. That was as much as he'd done to get ready to leave. His friend Fred was standing near him.

"Audra," Fred said, "you've been here a few days now. Feeling like an old hand?"

She nodded. "I think I'm remembering everything." She wanted to remind them that her first day hadn't really been her first day.

"My granddaughter is good at everything she does," Grandpa Paul said, "except bathing dogs."

Audra rolled her eyes. One sopping dog tearing through the house leaving soapy puddles and they wouldn't let her forget it. "I was eleven," she said.

Grandpa was chuckling and so was Fred, who had probably heard the story ten times.

"Well, she is talented," Fred said. "I've wandered next door to appreciate your paintings a few times, but I keep forgetting to do it on a Saturday so you can sell me one."

"Oh, you could have one for free," Audra said.

Fred shook his head and spoke forcefully, "No, I could not. I will not take advantage of my friendship with your grandfather to cheat you out of hard-earned money."

"Um… okay." Audra sensed that agreement was the only option. She was pretty sure his friendship with her grandfather was the only reason he wanted a painting so she felt she was the one taking advantage. But he sounded as though he'd be offended if she didn't just agree with him.

"Glad we have that settled." Fred's expression softened. "Now, what kind of plans do you have for the weekend? I hope you'll be doing something fun with a special young man."

"No," Audra said. "I'll probably do some painting on Sunday, but that will be *alone*." She emphasized the word, hoping he got the point that there was no special young man in her life.

"I see," Fred said. "You haven't decided yet which of your admirers you're going to make the luckiest man on the planet." He smiled teasingly, but there was sadness in his eyes.

Fred had lost his wife of forty-six years less than a year ago. Audra guessed that he was thinking of his late wife and sympathy tied up her tongue.

Her grandfather didn't appear to have the same affliction. He chimed in with, "She and Logan haven't shared their wedding plans with the rest of us yet."

"What!?" Audra said.

"Logan?" Fred looked thoughtful. "The Fuller kid?"

Grandpa Paul nodded.

"Grandpa," Audra said, "I'm not dating Logan."

"Uh-huh." He sounded as though he didn't believe her and shared a knowing look with Fred.

"I'm not," Audra repeated. "In fact, he's going out with Violet tomorrow."

Grandpa Paul tipped his head as though he didn't understand what she was saying. "Why would he do that?" he asked.

"Because..." Audra stopped herself from saying because she asked him to. That felt wrong somehow. Instead, she said, "What's wrong with Violet?"

"Nothing." Grandpa Paul shrugged, looking amused.

"Well, I guess I'll mosey on out of here," Fred said.

Audra smiled, happy for the subject change. "Have a nice weekend," she said.

He nodded and lifted his hand in a wave to Grandma May, who was behind the counter with her purse already over her shoulder.

"Looks like your grandmother is ready to go," Grandpa said. "I'll see you on Monday."

Audra had spoken to her grandma before she went to get an apron. She called out a farewell to both of them and went to work straightening a few chairs until a customer entered. The place wasn't completely empty again before it filled up with the lunch crowd.

The noon hour was already Audra's favorite time at the restaurant. She thrived on the adrenaline of rushing from table to table. The place was noisy, but it was a happy noise. There were a few families. Most of the customers were people who worked in town and spent regular lunches there. They called out greetings to the others they recognized and sometimes even had conversations from neighboring tables.

One person that Audra recognized was the woman she'd been watching when she came to talk to Ryan. She looked a little older than Audra but still under thirty. She had golden brown hair, a bit darker by the roots, and glasses with tortoise-shell frames. The woman had been there for lunch on Tuesday, Wednesday, Thursday and now Friday. Each day she kept her nose in a book except for regular glances at the door.

Audra still wanted to believe she was waiting for some romantic rendezvous. But it was difficult to attach romance to being stood up repeatedly. Plus, Audra had noticed she usually let her shoulder-length hair fall in front of her face as she looked up. It appeared she might be watching for someone she did not necessarily want to see her. The situation made Audra so curious she couldn't stand it any longer.

Since the woman had started her lunch a bit later that day than she had the rest of the week, the crowd had thinned by the time she finished. Audra decided to ask. Maybe getting yelled at to mind her own business would be better than dying of curiosity. She was already committed before she realized that she still wouldn't know anything.

"Hi. No hurry with this." Audra set the check on the table. "Forgive me if I'm out of line, but I couldn't help noticing that you've been watching the door, and I wondered if there's anything I could help with. I mean, I'm here a lot so maybe…" Maybe what? With no idea what she was looking for, Audra had no ideas on how to help. She simply left the offer incomplete.

The woman gave a nervous laugh and said, "You can tell I'm watching for someone?"

Audra nodded, then tried to reassure her that it wasn't weird and neither was Audra watching her watch for someone. "But it's my job to pay attention to customers to see when they might need me. I'm sure no one else noticed."

Her eyes swept the room behind Audra for proof of oblivious patrons. "I'm just hoping to solve a little mystery."

"A mystery?" Audra knew she'd been given a vague answer because that was all the customer wanted to share. But it was a deliciously intriguing vague answer. She fought to keep quiet for a brief pause, just in case there was a change of heart.

Instead of offering more information, the woman pulled a credit card from a small bag at her side.

"Okay," Audra said, trying very hard not to sound disappointed. "I'll be right back." She went through the kitchen on her way to the register, even though that was a longer route. She wondered if it would make a difference to return to the table at a time to catch her looking up at someone opening the door.

Audra didn't ask again and didn't hear anything else about the mystery. She managed to put it out of her head most of the rest of her time at work. But sometime after she rushed home to meet Violet, Alison and Elaine for Tichu, she was faced with a new mystery. Why did it seem that a 61-year-old woman didn't know how to count?

"Steps have to be consecutive pairs," Audra said, pointing to the threes and sevens Elaine had played.

"Oops." Elaine put the cards back into her hand and stared at it.

Audra was trying to be patient. There was a lot to learn in Tichu, and Elaine was still a beginner. But that was the third time she'd explained steps in one game. Audra's effort to be patient won even if she and Elaine did not. She ended the game still smiling at her partner.

Elaine smiled back. "I suppose we need to visit the young men next door now?"

"They would miss us so much if we didn't," Alison said.

"Some of them would miss some of you," Elaine said more seriously. "That's another reason I need to be replaced with someone younger."

Alison put an arm around her mom's shoulders as they moved towards the door. "We'll get you out of this if we can, Mom, but don't say we're replacing you. Just giving you the option to watch."

Violet got to the guys' door first and rang the bell before she opened it. She smiled at Audra, knowing who would get the blame for the noise.

Audra laughed when she came in with Trevor already shaking his head at her. There was no point in trying to convince anyone she hadn't rung the bell, especially since she would have if Violet hadn't gotten there first. She just went over to check the score. "Ouch!" she said. "You guys are negative."

"Cameron went big in the first round with a Grand Tichu," Logan said. "We're still trying to recover, but it isn't hopeless."

Cameron shrugged sheepishly. "It seemed solid at the time."

"At least you aren't on Ryan's team," Audra said. "He'd still be yelling at you."

"What?" Ryan looked up from his cards. "Why am I the bad guy?"

"He was yelling at everyone today," Audra said.

"I didn't *yell* at anyone," he said, then folded up the rest of his hand as he was the only one not out.

"That might help us catch up," Cameron observed.

Ryan wasn't finished defending himself. "We have a few high school kids who come in after school, and I'm gonna sound like such an old man when I say this but... some of them can't keep their hands off their phones. One girl stopped in the middle of taking someone's order to reply to several texts. I had to tell her that she could interrupt conversations with her friends if they don't mind, but it's not acceptable at work. Customers get your full attention. And Ben?" He sighed and shook his head. "The kid cannot get it through his thick skull that he contaminates himself every time he touches something not related to food prep. I have to send him to rewash his hands every time he pulls the germy phone from his pocket. There were other times today, too. But I didn't yell."

"Sounds like he deserved it," Violet said.

He grunted agreement, then held his hand out to Logan, who was absently shuffling the cards. "It's my deal, isn't it?"

"Huh? Oh, right." Logan passed him the cards.

Alison and Elaine were, as usual, content to say hello. They left before Ryan finished the deal.

Logan held his cards up to Audra. "Do you want to play this

round while *I* stand behind *you* wincing and gasping and giving away the cards?"

"I am not that bad," she said.

"I could even point things out as though you're blind."

"I have never done that."

He raised his eyebrows skeptically.

Audra thought about it. "Okay. I pointed once," she said. "But I didn't think you didn't see it. I was only trying to share in something good."

"You were sharing that I had something good with the whole table," Logan said. He had begun to sort his cards, making it clearer he'd been joking about letting her play.

"I'm glad I don't have to worry about Violet's poker face," Ryan said.

Violet took a step from Audra to be more directly behind Ryan, then let her mouth fall open in exaggerated shock.

"Very funny," he said. He kept his tone dry but the corners of his mouth were fighting a laugh.

Violet cranked up the reaction with a loud gasp and a hand over her heart. Light laughter came from all the guys, including Ryan.

"The only problem," Trevor said, "is that I can't tell if that means he has something really good or really bad."

"Honestly, it's what I want to do every time I see a hand sorted backwards," Violet said.

"Backwards?" Logan asked.

Audra leaned over to see what she meant, but her brother flattened his cards against his chest before she could see them.

"He puts the high cards on the left," Violet explained.

"That's not backwards," Logan said.

"What?"

"Yeah, I'm in the high cards on the left camp, too," Trevor said.

"You guys are wrong," Cameron said. "I'm with Violet. You count from left to right so the cards should increase from left to right."

"But you don't count the cards, you *rank* them," Logan said.

Trevor shook his head. "You should always count the cards so you know if they've been dealt properly."

"Only if you're the dealer," Logan countered.

Audra was entertained by the seriousness of the guys' debate.

Violet appeared more cautious. "I didn't mean to start anything," she said.

"It's fine," Ryan said. "But now that we know the *right* way to sort the cards, can we start playing?"

They'd managed to pass cards while talking and began to look at each other expectantly. Audra could see the starting card in Logan's hand. The other guys focused on him, and she wasn't sure if they noticed he was staring into space or if they really could read something on her face. This was one time it didn't matter so she poked his arm.

Logan turned his eyes to her only briefly before he focused on playing the round. In that moment, Audra felt… something. Was it contentment he communicated? His eyes seemed to say he was happy where he was, surrounded by friends and even being poked by one of them. But there was also a question, perhaps a suggestion that she try harder to be at peace with the relationship as well.

Audra was washed away in a flood of memories. There was a service project at church. They were packing boxes of food, and the youth leaders had turned it into a contest to see which side of the room could pack more boxes. Audra had been rushing so much she knocked a stack of soup cans off the table. Logan hit the floor before she had time to panic, chasing the rolling cans back to her to keep their assembly line moving. She remembered being in a dark movie theater with him. Her brothers had been on either side of them, but it was the only time the four of them saw a movie without either Ryan or Trevor between them. The time felt special even though the movie wasn't. Audra remembered the first time she went bowling with the guys. She'd tried it with her parents and some friends but was still terrible. Logan had tried to give her some pointers. There was incredible tension as he seemed to constantly come close to touching her hands before stopping himself. It was one of the few times she remembered overtly flirting with him, nearly every time her brothers were looking another way. They were playing a much faster game in the next lane.

The sound of cards shuffling brought Audra back to the present. Logan, of course, was the one doing the shuffling. Violet was laughing at something someone had said, a slightly nervous laugh. Audra shoved the memories of hope aside to be in the moment. No one appeared to have noticed her mental absence, though she avoided looking too closely at Logan.

They enjoyed a bit of conversation over the last few hands — mostly between the hands as the guys preferred to concentrate — then it was time to call it a night. Cameron was the first to the door. Logan teased him about rushing out to check his correspondence. Audra noticed that Cameron only waved. He didn't deny anything. She wanted to stay outside and talk to Logan, see if she could get more information — or at least speculation — about this potential romance. But she didn't want Violet to misinterpret anything. She simply told Logan she'd see him tomorrow before she followed Violet into their apartment. Audra tried not to think that tomorrow might be difficult. She could not have predicted the actual events anyway.

8

*A*lison and Elaine had a game set up on a table near the back when Audra arrived at Next Love. It wasn't something she had played before.

"Do you want to be red penguins or blue?" Alison asked.

Audra knew she was being invited to play, but she still had to laugh at the odd greeting. "Why am I turning into penguins?"

"That's how you get the fish," Elaine said. "And by the way, good morning."

Alison held out little wooden penguins, blue in one hand, red in the other.

Audra took the red ones. "Are you expecting a slow day?"

"We'll have to pause every time someone comes in." Alison gestured to her work corner. "But I've been super productive this week so I'm giving myself a light day on the project side."

"She's earned it," Elaine said.

Audra didn't doubt it. Both women put in long hours to keep the family business running so it was nice that they brought some fun with them from time to time. And nice that they included Audra. The first customer came in before they'd finished explaining the rules though. Alison continued while her mom went to discuss furniture.

The game was quick once they got started. They played twice with only a few interruptions. The Brachys had a little wooden frog as a turn marker. It was a strange figurine with wings that they had dubbed Fly Frog. He was passed around the board as they took turns so they could keep track even if someone took a turn while someone else was busy. Audra turned the funny little frog over in her hands before she set it aside.

Elaine had won the first game and Alison the second. They had both agreed to play a third time before they were called away by the repeatedly opening door. Audra began to set up the pieces to start over. She thought she was getting the hang of it and would have a better chance the next time. As it appeared the other players would be busy for a while, she was taking her time laying out the board. Then the front door opened yet again.

The man who entered was carrying a canvas. Audra assumed that it was one of her paintings and that he was there to talk to her about it. She got up and walked towards her wall of work to meet him halfway. Perhaps the painting had been scratched or damaged in some way. Of course she would fix it for him if she could. No charge. It occurred to her in the moment that she'd be willing to offer that service but not mention it upfront to anyone. There was no need to encourage people to be careless with her artwork. But she would do her best to help those who asked.

She smiled at him as they got closer, though she remembered the painting in his hand more than she remembered him. "Hello, sir," she said. "How are you today?"

"I'm fine. Thanks." He held the painting up between them. "You're the one who sold me this, right?"

Audra nodded. "Yes."

"Good," he said. "I'd like to return it."

"Uh… what?"

"I'd like to return it," he repeated.

Audra had heard him the first time, but she still didn't know how to respond. She had not expected this. Her brain searched for professional words. "Is… is something wrong with it?"

He shrugged. "Nah. We're just tired of looking at it already."

"Tired of looking at it." Audra felt her mouth form the words she was struggling to process. Why she thought saying them out loud would help, she didn't know. She took the painting he handed her and stared at it.

"So can I have my money back?" he asked.

Audra looked up again feeling lost. She supposed she would have to return his money, but how? She hadn't sold any paintings that day and therefore didn't have enough cash in her purse. She certainly didn't have *his* money. She didn't know what to do.

"Please," he added. "I'd like to use it to buy something that doesn't make my wife sigh whenever she walks into the room."

"Wait here," Audra said. She carried the painting with her as she walked away before she knew where she was going. She needed help. Alison and her mom were both talking to customers. Audra walked to the back room and peeked inside. Alison's dad was running an electric sander. He was covered in sawdust and safety goggles and noise. She closed the door before he even noticed her.

Still carrying the painting, she approached Elaine. "I'm sorry," she said. "Can I interrupt for a minute?"

"Sure thing." Elaine addressed her customer. "I'll be right back if you'll excuse me."

The woman she'd been helping didn't seem to mind. She nodded politely as Elaine ushered Audra a few feet away.

"What do you need?" Elaine asked.

"He wants to return this."

Elaine glanced at the man waiting for Audra. "You'd be within your rights to say that sales are final."

"I know," she said. She sort of knew it, but she wasn't sure she believed it. "I don't have enough money with me."

Elaine nodded with an understanding and very motherly expression. "Come with me." She led Audra to the cash register and pulled out enough money for the refund. She knew Audra sold all her paintings for the same amount. "I trust you to pay us back with the next sale, which I know might even be later today."

Audra took the money gratefully but couldn't quite accept the reassurance. "Thank you."

The man was wearing a white dress shirt and khaki pants. He might have been running the errand during a break in his workday. His shirt was tucked crookedly in the back, which Audra could see because he was facing the wall, pretending to be interested in her other paintings. She summoned her most polite smile as he faced her again and tried not to wish someone in his office was laughing that he couldn't properly dress himself.

"Here you go," she said. "I'm sorry it didn't work for you."

"Yeah, I thought we'd like it, too." He pulled a wallet from his pocket to insert the cash as he spoke. "Have a nice day."

Audra watched him leave, keeping her smile plastered to her face in case he looked back. He did not. She sighed and headed back to the game she'd left. The returned painting was still in her hand. She couldn't explain why she didn't hang it up to sell to someone else. It just felt tainted somehow. She leaned it against a table leg before she resumed setting up fish tiles.

The customer Alison had been helping left, and she'd apparently been multitasking her attention. She walked up to Audra and said, "Did that man actually have the nerve to come in here and ask you for a refund?"

"Yes." Audra almost smiled at the indignation radiating off her friend on her behalf.

"I'd suggest you write all sales final on your sign," Alison said, "except that some people always think they're the exceptions anyway."

"That's what your mom said. Well, the part about no refunds."

Alison nodded. "I doubt it'll come up again so it probably isn't necessary to have a policy."

"Thanks," Audra said. She didn't want to talk about it though. "I think I got the strategy of this now. Can we play with just the two of us or should we wait for your mom?"

Alison looked over her shoulder to study the scene in the showroom. Elaine was talking to a woman around her age, laughing while the other woman said something about how long it took someone to notice something. "Sounds like a chatty one," Alison diagnosed. "Let's do one without her. It's quick."

****

Audra left the returned painting in her car when she got home. She hadn't decided what to do with it, and she didn't want Violet to ask her why she couldn't sell it again.

Violet was pulling some sliced turkey from the fridge when she came in. "I'm going to have a sandwich for lunch," she said. "Do you want one?"

"Sure. Be right back." Audra ducked into her room and tossed her purse onto her bed. She changed into sitting around the apartment clothes and went to wash her hands.

Violet had a spread of fixings on the table by the time she returned and was already assembling her own sandwich next to some fresh pineapple. "How many did you sell today?" she asked.

"I did sell one just before I left actually," Audra said. It was the truth, but it didn't feel like the truth when she didn't mention it raised her net sales to zero. She slapped some bread on a plate and tried to sound cheerful. "Are you looking forward to learning how to bowl?"

Violet smiled because she knew Audra wasn't really asking about bowling. "Yes," she said. "But I'm also very nervous."

"It'll be fine," Audra said. "Great, I mean. It'll be great."

"Are you sure you..." Violet stopped and sucked in her lower lip. She was clearly trying to ask something she feared having answered.

Audra guessed it had something to do with making sure she didn't still have feelings for Logan that would get in the way, but addressing that again would only make Violet suspect that she protested too much. She only said, "Trust me."

Violet nodded. She was trying to suppress a big grin and chew at the same time. She seemed to swallow some nerves with the bite. "I guess it will at least be very... casual. Right?"

"It doesn't get much more casual than Beehive Lanes," Audra said. On a Saturday afternoon, it would likely be full of hyper kids and the commotion of the bumpers going up and down when it was their parents' turns. With the usual noise of pins, too. "It's not as though I'm setting you up for a dreamy moonlight picnic or something."

"Yeah. I would not have agreed to anything with romantic pressure." Violet laughed and seemed satisfied with the plan now that a worse one had been dismissed.

They had a fairly inconsequential chat as they finished eating and cleared the table. Audra wanted to be alone with her thoughts afterwards so she got out her sketchpad. She rarely drew scenes before she painted them, but something about staring at the blank page helped her visualize possibilities. It didn't work that day. All she could see on the paper was the ocean scene she'd already painted, the one sitting in the back seat of her car. She kept trying to picture ways she might have made it better, changes that might have kept someone from getting tired of looking at it.

The words sounded more insulting every time she ran them through her head. The next minute she'd tell herself she was making a mountain out of a molehill. Lots of people had come into the store, looked at her paintings, and left without taking one home. That didn't bother her. Why should taking one home only for a little while hurt her feelings? Maybe because the man had been completely unapologetic. Maybe because he had no idea that she poured a tiny piece of herself into each work, that saying his wife sighed at the sight of it was like saying she sighed at Audra's very existence.

Again with the mountain. Audra was trying to accept the hurt and move on, but the contrast of happiness in the background wasn't helping. Violet had started a video call with her mom and sister. They were looking at wedding invitations, and it sounded as though they were having just as much fun disparaging the designs they didn't like as they were admiring the ones they did.

Audra put away her sketchpad and took her phone outside. She sat on the front step to call her own mom. That would be just the pick-me-up she needed. "Hey, Mom," she said. "How are you doing?"

"Good, good. One of my clients mentioned seeing your work on display yesterday. You're quickly becoming the most famous artist in town." She gave a little chuckle because she knew that wasn't saying much and that Audra had no desire to really be famous anyway.

"That's nice," Audra said, mostly because she preferred the idea of her mom talking about her work with her clients rather than her personal life. Her mom was a hair dresser. Logan's mom was one, too. They no longer worked at the same salon, but it was how the families knew each other in the first place.

"I bet you sold a few more today," her mom said. "Didn't you?"

"One."

"All right! I knew it." The tone made Audra imagine her waving her arms in a celebratory cheer. "And how's Alison? Still smitten with my boy?"

"We don't talk about Trevor, Mom."

"But you were so happy to help orchestrate…"

"That was before they were together," Audra cut in. "Now I don't need to hear about it. They're on their own."

"She's so nice. I know she's the one for him and not just because I think it's time my kids got hitched."

Audra felt herself rolling her eyes. They immediately transitioned to talking about her and Ryan starting at the January Café again. It seemed all her mom wanted to talk about lately was how "all her babies were turning into grownups." They'd all had jobs for years and the relationship was sort of new but still not the direction Audra wanted to steer the conversation. Not that she really wanted to backtrack to the disappointment of having a painting returned.

She listened patiently while her mom babbled on and then assured her she'd stop by for her dad's birthday dinner later in the week. Audra hung up with her feelings less boosted than she'd hoped. The sound of a car alerted her to Logan parking in front of the house. Was it 2 o'clock already?

9

*L*ogan was a few minutes early. When he saw Audra sitting on the front steps, he figured he was right on time.

She said, "hello," and smiled as he walked up the sidewalk, but he could see in her eyes that something was wrong.

"Are you okay?" he asked.

She shrugged and dropped her eyes to her feet.

Logan couldn't tell if the shrug meant it was not a big deal or that she didn't want to talk about it. He sat down next to her and nudged her shoulder with his. She nudged him back with a smile, a small smile and wet eyelashes. Time to rule out no big deal. "What's going on?"

"I… I'm afraid if I tell you, I'll start crying," she said. "And then I'll be embarrassed because it's not worth crying over." She hadn't looked up yet, but he could tell her eyes had started leaking before she swiped her fingers across her cheek.

Since it was too late to stop the crying, he pressed the question. "Go ahead and tell me," he said.

Audra gave an annoyed sigh, which was better than sad at least. "Someone returned a painting today."

"What do you mean?"

"This guy who bought one of my paintings… I don't know, maybe a few weeks ago… He came in today and asked for his money back."

"You didn't give it to him, did you?"

Her eyes finally left the sidewalk and turned on him flashing with anger. "Why does everyone keep telling me I should have made him keep the painting he didn't want?"

"Uh…" Logan took little consolation from not being the first person to say that very wrong thing. It might be a good idea to get more information before he said anything else. "What did he say?"

"He said he was tired of looking at it and that his wife sighs every time she sees it."

"And what did you say?" Logan asked. He wanted to suggest that was when she punched the guy, but he thought it was best to keep his questions as matter-of-fact as possible while her mood was volatile.

"I don't remember exactly what I said. I think I just stared at him all dumbstruck for a few seconds." The explanation continued without further prompting, and, luckily, the tears dried up once the words started flowing. "It was awful because I wanted to give the money quickly so he'd leave, but I didn't have enough and had to borrow some from Elaine, which was so humiliating. I'm supposed to keep my finances separate. That's the whole reason I have to be there to sell them. And I'm just so glad I was able to pay her back before I left so it's not on my conscience all week."

He nodded. "You must have sold one after –"

"Yes," she said, sounding as though he was the one who had interrupted her. "The day wasn't all bad. I played a few games with Alison and Elaine, too. I don't know why I'm letting the return get to me so much."

"Hey, are you sure you don't want to come bowling? You could picture the guy's face on all the pins."

A genuine smile appeared before she shook her head and said, "Not this time. Tomorrow will be my first chance to paint in like a week and a half, and I'm fresh out of ideas. So that's what I'll be doing while you're gone."

"Wow. I should totally be offended that you're choosing staring at a blank piece of paper over spending time with me."

She laughed. "It's more fun than it sounds."

"I don't believe you," he said, "but I am looking forward to seeing what you come up with so I guess I'll let it go."

"You…" Audra had a strange expression. "I almost believe *you.*"

What was with the wistful tone? Did she honestly not believe he enjoyed seeing her art? "Why are you saying almost?"

Her mouth started to form a word, then maybe a different one. Neither had any sound to tell him what she might be trying to say or thinking about. Logan was thinking that she was very close and that watching her mouth was very tempting. He moved closer, and she did not back away. He moved all the way in to a kiss. There was a definite response.

At first, it was the sweet bliss of her kissing him back.

But then she was on her feet before he knew she was pulling away. "What was that!?" she hissed, eyes stretched as wide as they could possibly go.

Logan stood up slowly, dazed and trying to figure out where to go from there. She was clearly in shock because she knew what a kiss was. Shock was probably the last emotion he would have expected though. He was sure he'd been telegraphing a desire to do that for a very long time. And she just sat there and let him.

"That did *not* just happen." Audra scanned the area as though an absence of witnesses would make her statement true.

"Yes, it did," he said.

She put her fingers on her lips, not in an action of wiping anything away but as though she could still feel it and that was getting in the way of her disbelief.

Good. It had been a powerful moment. It still was, and the fact that she felt something was more important than whatever crazy words were coming out of her mouth.

"No." She said it forcefully, then checked the time. "You have a date with Violet in two minutes."

"What!?" The surprise actually sent him a step backwards. And unlike Audra, he was entitled to be shocked. No one said anything about a date. They were going bowling. Audra had been invited to come along, more than once. It wasn't a date.

Audra stepped closer, keeping her voice low and almost threatening. "You can never tell anyone what you just did. You're going to honor this commitment, and if things don't work out with you and Violet, it can*not* have anything to do with me."

"Audra, it has everything to do with you. I can't..."

She didn't let him finish. "Yes, you can," she said. "Don't hurt her, and please don't make me. I'm going to see my brothers. She doesn't even have to know you talked to me on the way in." Audra was already moving away as she spoke. She disappeared around the corner leaving emptiness and confusion.

****

Logan stared at Audra's front door knowing she wasn't behind it. That seemed to be the only stable thought in his head. Was he really about to take out one woman in order to make the one he loved happy? What kind of twisted situation had he gotten himself into? Would it really make Audra happy? He was swimming in a mess of dangerous what the heck.

Surely Violet didn't think this was a date. That seemed to be where he had to start. Audra had made it clear she'd be mad at him if Violet got hurt. The first thing he had to do was take Violet bowling and convince her it wasn't a date and that there was nothing but friendship between them while not saying anything that might hurt her feelings and then have her be the one to explain to Audra that he'd successfully done that. Simple. Yeah, right. He wasn't kidding himself even a little. He had no idea how to do any of that.

He raised his arm to knock. He wasn't going to figure it out so he might as well get started screwing it up.

"Hi," Violet said as she opened the door. Then she looked behind him. "I thought Audra was out here."

"She went to her brothers' place." Logan remembered as the words left his mouth that he wasn't supposed to tell Violet he'd seen Audra. That was progress. He was already screwing up.

Violet smiled nervously as she looked towards the corner where Audra had disappeared. "I guess we should go then?"

"Yeah, if you're ready," he said.

She nodded and came outside to lock the door behind her. It took longer than it should have to walk to Logan's car because she kept looking back around the side of the house. She didn't seem to expect him to open the door for her or anything, which of course meant nothing.

Logan walked around to get behind the wheel. He started the car for what should be a short drive. Beehive Lanes was only about a mile and a half away.

"So," Violet said. "Bowling. I know the idea is to knock down all the pins. Any trick to that?"

"You want to aim for the center," Logan said, even though it wasn't a trick. It was obvious.

"Yeah, that makes sense," Violet said. Because it was obvious. "Audra was trying to help me. She told me the hardest part was how heavy the ball is, but she also told me about a time she accidentally threw it into the next lane. I don't understand how she could throw it that far if it's so heavy. She was also telling me her interpretation of scorekeeping even though the computer does it for you and..." Violet kept talking about Audra's advice.

Logan was smiling at the memory of Audra making him come with her to apologize when she knocked over pins in the next lane. Until he realized how much Violet was babbling. She sounded nervous, like a person on a date.

How!? How had he done this to himself. Logan thought back to the conversation where Audra suggested he teach Violet to bowl. He'd been very quick to agree. Like every time Audra asked him to do something, he'd asked how high and not if it was a trap. Was this the reason Audra had turned him down, because Violet was interested? How was he supposed to kill Violet's hopes without killing his hopes with Audra?

Audra was already mad. He pictured the fire in her eyes when she told him to never tell anyone what *he'd* done, as though she hadn't been a willing participant in that kiss. Logan kind of wanted to yell out for the record that none of this mess was his fault. But if he examined that record too closely, he'd have to admit he'd been an idiot not to realize how going somewhere alone with Violet might look. If she went home disappointed after this, it would be at least partly his fault.

The feeling that a beautiful gift had been given and then snatched away was as distracting as it was distressing. Logan hadn't heard half of what Violet said on the way there. Not listening was not going to help him not be a jerk. He tried to focus on Violet as they got out of the car. This wasn't her fault either.

"You know, I actually drive past this place on my way to work every day," Violet said. "Now I'll be able to picture the inside as I go by."

Logan nodded at the observation and pulled the door open for her. It was polite no matter the circumstances.

She smiled as she entered. The air was already heavy with music and voices. Pins crashed as she turned around to wait for him. "By the way, thanks for doing this," she said. "I mean, I know you're doing it for Audra, but still."

Now he was glad he was paying attention not only because it was the respectful thing to do but because what she'd just said sounded important. "Wait a minute." He stopped walking before he got to the counter.

Violet also stopped and looked at him expectantly.

How could he get her to elaborate without putting his foot in his mouth? Perhaps the best way to avoid saying something stupid was to repeat what she said. "You know I'm doing this for Audra?"

"You'd do just about anything for her, wouldn't you?"

Was that a trick question? Fortunately, it was rhetorical.

Violet kept talking without waiting for an answer. "It's sweet. I know she'd do the same so I don't understand why…" She threw up her hands. "But that's none of my business."

Logan resumed the walk feeling *almost* relieved. It sounded as though Violet was well aware of how he felt about Audra and not bothered by it. She couldn't possibly… But why would Audra think it was a date if Violet didn't? Something still didn't quite add up.

Violet offered to pay for half, and he didn't argue. It was fair because the person who issued the invitation wasn't there to pay. They were assigned lane eight. Disappointment flashed across her face as Violet located that lane. But maybe that was Logan's imagination because the lane assignment didn't matter. If it did, they'd gotten a good one. It was on the side by the door and not the noisier side by the arcade.

They sat down to change their shoes. Even if he wasn't completely relaxed, Logan was less panicky and prepared to make the best of the time. He did enjoy bowling. Violet may not have been the person he most wanted to be there, but she was perfectly nice. And she'd never played. He was pretty much guaranteed to win. "Do you want to go first?" he asked.

She was turned sideways to look at the door. Her eyes were the last to leave it as she turned back to Logan. "Uh… yeah. Yeah, I guess we should start."

"First we pick a ball." He pointed at the rack, wondering why she'd had to think about whether or not to start.

"Okay." She jumped up. "How do I do that?"

He accompanied her to the rack and slid his fingers into the holes of a ball. "You'll want one you can pick up and hold with one hand like this." There were a lot of kids there so she might have trouble finding a lighter one. She settled on one quickly though, saying she liked the blue swirls so perhaps weight wasn't her primary criterion.

She still seemed a little nervous and kept glancing at the door while he entered their names in the scoresheet. "Can I ask you a question?" she said.

"Yeah." Especially if it was about bowling.

"Why do you go by Logan and not Bartholomew?"

That was a story he'd told quite a few times but apparently not to Violet. "Because my parents made a mistake," he said.

She looked as though she wanted to laugh but wasn't sure she should.

That was the most common reaction. He continued the explanation. "My mom said they settled on Bartholomew immediately after they found out she was pregnant. They both liked it, and that was the end of the discussion. But then a few weeks after I was born, she decided that it was a huge mouthful for an infant. She didn't like Bart or any other nicknames she thought of so she started using my middle name. It stuck."

"Was it weird when you found out Logan wasn't your real name?" she asked, then winced. "I mean, it is your real name, but..."

Logon nodded. He knew what she meant because it had been a little weird. "I remember when I was in first grade, the teacher was reading the roll and said, 'Bartholomew Fuller.' I looked around to see who had the same last name as me. But no one raised a hand. Then at the end, she asked if there was anyone she didn't call. When I told her my name, she said, 'Oh. No one calls you Bartholomew.' I went home and asked my mom why the teacher thought anyone would call me that, and she explained how it was on all the official paperwork and that she kind of wished they had named me Logan Bartholomew instead. Anyway, I think that's why my brother's name is Jack. They learned the hard way they preferred short names. At least for boys."

Violet smiled at the story. She was obviously listening even though her eyes kept darting back to the entrance. Was she expecting someone?

He was just going to stick to bowling and not ask. "Okay, you're up," he said. He pointed out the fault line and demonstrated a basic swing.

Her first ball went in the gutter, but she started to get the hang of it quickly. She was naturally a bit more athletic than Audra. She did pretty well for a first time, and even got one strike. Logan still beat her though. She seemed to enjoy the game and stopped looking towards the door as often. By the end of the second game – which he also won – she was checking the time instead. And frowning at it. He wasn't too surprised when he asked if she wanted to play again and she shook her head.

"No. We should go."

They turned in the shoes and headed for his car. She was very quiet on the ride home. Logan was afraid something was wrong. If he thought he needed to clarify anything between them, he would have done that. He was sure that wasn't the issue though. Their time had been strictly platonic, a couple of fist bumps but no flirting. Violet had mentioned Audra a few times while they played, seemed to know he wouldn't mind talking about her. There had been no hints of jealousy. Violet was going to have to talk to Audra about whatever expectations hadn't been met. He'd only signed up for bowling.

"Well, thanks again," Violet said as he parked at the curb. "I did have fun. Bye." She sounded falsely bright and got out without inviting him to follow.

Logan had originally hoped to spend some time with Audra after the bowling, but it was best that he didn't now. She was probably still upset with him. Violet needed to go in there and explain what was bothering her and how it had nothing to do with him. Then he could talk to Audra. Then he could more than talk to her. Logan smiled at the memory of what had happened right before she got upset. He looked forward to repeating that without the yelling.

*A*udra hadn't really felt the dread of a Monday morning since school. That was the last time she'd had anything like a nine to five schedule. She didn't understand why she was feeling dread that Monday. She should have been glad to go back to work because she'd had an awful weekend.

It had started with that returned painting that hardly bothered her at all after everything else. She was still embarrassed that she'd had to borrow from the Brachys and planned to have enough cash to handle a return every Saturday from now on. That was annoying. But she'd just stopped in to rehang the painting – and check that the others were straight – and could hardly believe she'd cried over it.

Logan had caught her at that low moment. There was no excuse for what she'd done, but that didn't stop her from looking for one. She wished there was consolation in the fact that Violet didn't know what had happened. She told Logan not to tell her and trusted him to keep his word, but he must have delivered some version of letting her down easy. Audra had stayed at her brothers' until after dinner, and Violet had already been shut in her room for the night when she came home. Sunday had been abnormally quiet, with only necessary and polite but stilted comments. It seemed neither of them wanted to talk about the date so they hardly talked about anything.

And the uncomfortable silence hadn't helped Audra's painting. Having still not thought of a nature scene she wanted to capture, she tried yet again to add people to her work. She made them small, trying to imagine they would eventually be at the top of a snow-covered hill. Even from a distance, the eyes looked sad. Even with smiles, the eyes looked sad. When she tried to compare them to real people to figure out whether it was the angle or the position or… why did they look sad? The only eyes she could summon to mind were Logan's expression when she told him the kiss didn't happen and Violet's eyes trying not to betray her sadness.

Three hours of trying to paint had left her with a lot of messy tools and no new picture. Her favorite hobby had been nothing but a source of frustration. Audra planned to stop thinking about it completely while she was at work because she would only get more frustrated otherwise.

"Hello to my favorite grandchild!"

Audra smiled at the sound of her grandma's voice filling the restaurant, in part because she knew she'd yelled the same thing when Ryan arrived. Grandma May was a tiny woman with a plain style to her hair and clothes. But her joyfulness stood out. Audra wished she could copy those sparkling eyes with paint, until she remembered not to think about that.

"Hi, Grandma," she said. The restaurant was mostly empty so she answered the greeting before she was quite at the counter. "How was your weekend?"

"It was…"

"Tell her about the surprise," Grandpa Paul cut in. He was clearing off his back table. Fred and John had presumably just left, unless he'd spent a lot of time talking to his wife before he got around to taking their coffee mugs to the kitchen.

"It wasn't a surprise," Grandma May said. "It was a last-minute idea that doesn't count for what you think it does."

He stacked the cups in one hand and came to stand next to her. "It was a last-minute stroke of genius, you mean. Got her a birthday surprise, and it only took me fifty-one years to do it."

Audra was confused. It was kind of a running joke that he always tried and failed to surprise Grandma May for her birthday. But her birthday wasn't until next month.

"If you're thinking that my birthday isn't for another month," Grandma May said, "you've caught on to why the supposed surprise doesn't count." She put her hands on her hips and angled away from the counter to face him. "You can't bring me flowers in September and say it's for my birthday in October."

"It was the same day of the month as your birthday, which proves I was thinking of you. And you didn't see it coming so it was a surprise."

Grandma May smiled almost despite herself. "The flowers *are* pretty. But you're not off the hook for my birthday present."

"I'm off the hook for the surprise part," he said, starting to walk towards the kitchen. "That's all I care about."

Audra laughed along with her grandma at the self-satisfied air.

Then Grandma May leaned her arm against the counter. "So how was *your* weekend?"

"Well, I didn't get flowers."

An interested eyebrow went up. Audra had only meant to say her weekend wasn't as noteworthy, but it appeared her grandma was reading more into the statement. "You and Logan aren't having trouble, are you?" she asked.

"Not possible," Audra said. "There'd have to be a me and Logan in order for us to have trouble."

Grandma May still had an expectant look, as though she was patiently waiting to hear about the trouble.

"I am not dating Logan."

"If you say so," she said.

Audra sighed and changed the subject. "I was just hoping to get a new painting done this weekend, and I couldn't even think of an idea."

"Sunset," Grandma May answered simply.

"I've already done a few sunsets."

"God does one every night, and no one ever gets tired of looking at them."

Audra was saved from stating the obvious, that she wasn't God, as Grandpa Paul returned. "Your paintings are beautiful even when you insist on making them kooky," he stated, with no room for argument. "Come on, May, we best make tracks for home."

Grandma May nodded and went to collect her things. Audra followed her to put on an apron to start the day. Ryan asked her to restock a few things, which he managed to do without sounding too bossy so she complied. It probably would have only taken her a minute to notice it needed to be done anyway. Her first customer of the day arrived right as she finished.

Among the regular lunch crowd was the woman Audra had interrogated on Friday. Audra approached her corner table still feeling curious but also somewhat contrite. "Hey," she said. "I'm glad you're back. I wanted to apologize for getting all nosy without even asking your name first."

"It's okay." She smiled in a way that said it really was okay. "I'm Katie, by the way."

"I'm Audra. I think I said that." She tapped her nametag. "And of course it's right here if I didn't."

"Well, you didn't scare me away," Katie said. "This is a great place for lunch even if I never solve my little mystery."

Audra's eyes involuntarily went to the front door at the mention. Perhaps if she and Katie became friendly enough, she'd find out what that was all about. But she wasn't going to ask today. Instead, she asked what she wanted to eat. It wasn't a mystery or a surprise since she had so far gotten the same thing every day.

She asked for it again on Tuesday. On Wednesday, however, Katie ordered something different.

"Whoa!" Audra exclaimed teasingly. "Are you sure you don't want your usual?"

Katie shook her head. "I overslept and didn't get much breakfast this morning. I need something more filling."

"Do you have to be at work very early?" Audra asked.

"8 o'clock. Do you have to be here at six?"

"No. I'm only here for lunch and dinner."

"Well, I know eight isn't early early, but I like to squeeze in a lot before I start work." Katie tipped her head thoughtfully. "Though maybe breakfast shouldn't be what I leave out when I'm rushed."

Audra shrugged. "I don't know. I assume everything else is important, too."

"I guess," Katie said. "Or maybe just harder to figure out how to shorten."

"Maybe. Are you still sure about going with the ham and cheese today? That's pretty bold."

Katie smiled. "I am. Though ruts are underrated."

"What?"

"Oh, something I read recently." She continued only after she checked to see if Audra was interested enough to stick around. "It was an article on, um, daily prayer."

Audra nodded encouragingly. She understood the hesitation of talking about prayer in front of a new acquaintance. It could end up like the guy at Mackenzie's who thought it was funny to joke that Audra talked to the "lowercase t" on her necklaces.

"It, uh, was about establishing routines to keep up the habit because it's easier to maintain once you are, well, in the rut."

"I can see that," Audra said. "Some people would call that getting into the groove, which – I've never thought about this before – but that's actually just a nicer word for rut."

Katie's expression was happy surprise. "It totally is."

"And I think they're underrated, too, so I'll expect you to go back to the taco salad tomorrow." She left the table still smiling, until a new customer caught her eye. Logan. He must have come in when her back was to the door. Katie probably saw him, but he wasn't connected to her mystery so the arrival would not have made *her* stomach clench and vibrate.

Audra went to the kitchen to put in Katie's order and take a breath or two before she approached Logan. "Hello, Mr. Fuller," she said. She hoped the formal greeting would sound droll and keep things from being tense. But it came out more stiff than formal.

"Miss Norman," he said. "I know you're busy, but can we talk for a minute?"

"It's part of my job to be friendly so I can make time for *banter.*"

His expression did a skeptical dance. It was clear he heard her saying she was only willing to chat lightly and was choosing to ignore that stipulation. "I only want to ask if you've worked everything out with Violet," he said.

"There's nothing to work out," Audra said. And she honestly believed it. Violet didn't know that Audra had interfered. She was upset that the date had gone poorly, but they really didn't need to talk about that. Violet just needed some time to forgive Audra for believing there could be a spark where there wasn't. Logan probably needed to forgive her for that, too. He'd appeared blindsided by the assertion that he had a date, though Audra didn't know how he could have missed the setup.

"Are you sure?" he asked.

She nodded, convincingly she hoped.

"Good." He exhaled slowly. "When am I going to see you next?"

"Probably Friday like always. Unless the girls and I are having too much fun to come over and interrupt your game."

"That's not what I meant."

She had guessed that by the tone, a tone that made her face warm. But she hoped to avoid this scene by taking it the neutral, non-romantic way. How many times had she fantasized about her relationship with Logan taking this turn? How could he possibly decide to make a move now that it was impossible for her to accept? "Logan, you can't... *I* can't do that to Violet."

"Violet?" He looked more confused than disappointed.

That helped to allay any concern over his feelings. He'd certainly be over this impulse by the time Violet was recovered. "Yes, Violet. I can just imagine telling her I'm going out with you while she's moping around."

Logan opened his mouth without immediately saying anything. His eyes darted around the restaurant, possibly taking in that it might not be the time or the place for the conversation she had tried not to have there. "Look," he said, "I'm sorry if Violet is upset about something, but I really don't think that's my fault."

"No, it's my fault," she said. "That's why I'm not going to do anything to make it worse. Now what do you want for lunch?"

He looked exasperated, as though she still wasn't understanding him. As stubborn as he was, this probably wasn't the end of the discussion. But he wisely chose to postpone it. "Hamburger," he said.

Audra nodded and walked away from his table. She only got in one more order before Katie's was ready. She set the sandwich with a side of fruit on the table. "Here you go. Do you need anything with this? Mustard maybe?"

Katie wrinkled her nose. "I would not have thought to put mustard on a grilled one, but... no, thanks. Do you have to work to keep a straight face with some of the things people ask for?"

"Yes," Audra said. "Not too often, but yes. I'll leave you to eat in peace unless you want to hear about some. Or unless you're ready to tell me about the mystery."

Audra was relieved when she got a laugh. She really wasn't trying to be pushy.

Katie nodded towards something over Audra's shoulder and

said, "Maybe someday soon I'll tell you about my mystery and you can tell me about yours."

She was referring to Logan, had noticed the tension in the exchange. It might have made Audra self-conscious if she hadn't picked up on the hint Katie had dropped. "Oh, wait," she said. "Does that mean your mystery involves a guy?"

A slow smile spread on Katie's face before she nodded.

"Enjoy your lunch," Audra said. She turned from the table feeling that Katie's story just got a little more interesting. Something else interesting was the two familiar faces that walked in together. It was the together part that was unexpected. Grandpa's friend Fred, the mild-mannered widower, was holding hands with Elaine's friend Sheila, the anti-romantic.

Audra shrank her eyes back to normal size before she greeted the pair. Neither of them acted as though there was anything weird about the situation, not that they should have. Audra's surprise didn't make her any less happy to see a budding relationship.

Katie finished without any developments on that front. Logan managed to stick to banter and light conversation the rest of his time there, some of it with Ryan. Fred left a ridiculous tip, more than the entire cost of their meal. Audra wasn't sure how to feel about that. When the crowd thinned, she went to the kitchen to get Ryan's take. He was on the phone.

"You can pick up your last check before the end of the week," he said. "I'll mail it if it's still here Monday." He hung up and looked at Audra.

"Who were you just talking to?" she asked.

"Becca."

"Did you just fire her?" Audra barely managed to keep her voice even.

Ryan only shrugged. "This is the third day in a row she hasn't shown up or called to say why. I think it's more accurate to say she quit without telling me, and I just let her know I figured it out."

Audra stared at him, wondering how that could sound perfectly reasonable and mean at the same time.

"Were you looking for me?"

"Oh, yes. Fred was here for lunch," she said.

"I saw him."

Audra glanced around to make sure none of the employees were close enough to overhear. "He left me something like a 500% tip. I can't keep that, and I can't give it back."

"Why can't you keep it?"

"Grandpa'd be mad," Audra said. "You know how the free morning coffee becomes a thing whenever Fred wants to get and pay for something to go with it."

"That's between them," Ryan said, waving a hand dismissively. "The tip is between you and Fred. I bet he enjoyed being generous and that he thinks you're smart enough not to mention it to Grandpa."

"Of course I'm not going to tell Grandpa," Audra said.

"Then why are you trying to make an issue of it?"

Audra couldn't answer that. At his incredulous tone, she began to think she'd only gotten worked up because other, more serious things were bothering her. Maybe she wanted to focus on something that could be fixed. Or something that didn't even need to be fixed. "Uh, yeah, I guess I hadn't quite thought it through."

Ryan was rolling his eyes as he walked away. Audra didn't say anything since it wasn't entirely undeserved. She was going to do better at staying calm and in the moment and mostly just thinking about Logan a lot less.

11

*A*udra was thinking about Logan when she arrived home. She sat in her car remembering Logan in the passenger seat. She hadn't driven him much, but she had given him a ride shortly after she bought the car. Though he'd been genuinely interested in checking it out, the new-to-her car had been a ruse on her part to get him alone. She had begun to seriously consider ending her time in college, and Logan was the first person she told.

He'd asked her a bunch of questions. None of them were reproachful of her choice. It was obvious he only wanted to be sure she'd considered all the angles. He'd offered to be with her when she told her parents. Audra had talked to them alone, but picturing Logan's support had helped. She called him afterwards and teased him about being an old man because her dad had asked many of the same questions.

Audra sighed as her thoughts coalesced around the present. Logan had always been easy to talk to about almost anything. Why hadn't she asked him if he had any interest in Violet before she set them up? Was she afraid he'd say he did? That didn't make sense. She wouldn't have tried to push them together if she wanted to avoid them being together. Was she afraid she might have influenced him by not masking her own feelings? She liked that explanation better than the idea that she'd cowardly wanted Logan to be the one to tell Violet it wouldn't work. Audra pushed her key into her lock and admitted she probably didn't talk to Logan first only because she'd been reckless.

Violet was sitting on the couch with a book. She looked up and nodded a greeting before her eyes went back to the page. There was music playing. Violet's Christian rock playlist had a lot of the same artists they heard on the radio but different songs.

Audra went into her bedroom, tossed her purse on a box by the door and bent over to untie her shoes. She stood still, taking in the cluttered room for a moment. A couple of boxes by her bed were open. Those were the clothes she wore most often. One box in a corner had most of the black stuff she used to wear to work. She had taped it up after her last day at Mackenzie's and put it under the box of random stuff from high school that her parents had insisted she take with her. She wasn't entirely sure what was in that box. How long would she hang on to either of them?

Her closet was fairly organized, especially by comparison. Finished paintings were on one side with drawers of supplies on the other. Audra's attention drifted to an 8 by 10 canvas on top of the dresser. It was blank, and it was smaller than all her other canvases. She had bought it on a whim, thinking it was the right size for a portrait.

But Audra didn't want to paint a portrait. She wanted to paint a whole scene. A scene with happy people, maybe playing Tichu, would be perfect. That was what Logan wanted. He wanted a painting with joy and action and memories and... anything but nature. Audra couldn't paint that. She couldn't paint people. She stared at the white surface trying to will an idea onto it.

She had already tried painting people far away. What if she painted them from the back? Could she make them appear happy by their movements? Kids skipping perhaps? What would make kids skip? Audra imagined a pair of brightly colored kites in a mostly clear sky. There was a wheatfield under it. The stalks were curved enough to show a gentle breeze, and they were nearly bursting with the anticipation of a full harvest. One in the foreground was a bit more yellow than the others. Because it was corn! Somewhere partially hidden in the sea of wheat was a miniature ear of corn, glimmering without its husk and… wait. Where were the kids holding those kite strings? Could she put them on a little hill in the background? Audra groaned and dissolved the picture. Even in her mind's eye the people looked like a sad afterthought. And kites were stupid.

Well, okay, kites were not stupid. Audra was only frustrated. She picked up her sketchbook and took it back to the main room of the apartment. It slapped against the kitchen table as she set it down. She was thinking about whether or not she wanted to try another idea. Audra wandered to the refrigerator and opened it. She already had dinner. She wasn't the least bit hungry or thirsty. She had no idea why she was looking inside the fridge. She closed the fridge and turned towards Violet. She was facing Violet but looking down at the sketchbook. They were not going to share a smile over the wayward move. Violet probably noticed. She knew Audra hadn't taken anything out. But she wasn't going to say anything about the restless and pointless opening of their refrigerator.

Audra resisted a sudden urge to open and close it again to demand a reaction. She sat at the table and flipped open the cover of her book. On a page half covered with doodles, she tapped her pencil point in time to the music and watched tiny dots appear. It was a good song, catchy and upbeat, but not energizing as it could have been. Violet typically cranked up her music when she worked out in the early evening. Judging by her damp hair, she had likely done that then showered and ate before she sat down to read. It was unusual for her to keep music playing while she read. Audra suspected it was an attempt to relieve the tense silence.

Why was it tense? Violet didn't want to talk about her failed date, and Audra didn't want to talk about her failed matchmaking. But that didn't mean they couldn't talk at all. The music wasn't that loud. Audra strode to the living room side of the room and plopped herself in the squishy chair opposite Violet. The chair was old and made a strange popping noise under the weight of a person. Audra liked it for its uniquely ugly brown pattern. The noise she didn't mind. "So…" she said.

Violet's eyes lifted expectantly.

"Did you end up shopping during your lunch break yesterday?"

Violet nodded and said, "Yeah."

One word. Audra paused in case there were more coming. Something in Violet's eyes said there were more, but she was uncertain about continuing.

"And did you find something?" Audra asked.

"Yes." Again there was only one word. But this time, after a brief hesitation, Violet closed her book and dropped one foot to the floor as though she was thinking about standing up. "Do you want to see it?"

"Yes, yes." Audra eagerly waved her roommate towards her bedroom. She'd been expecting another story about conflicting opinions. "If you picked out a dress, I definitely want to see it."

Violet smiled before she moved quickly into her room. She seemed happy to share. Audra tried to focus on that and not think she'd apparently had the dress more than twenty-four hours without sharing. When she returned, Violet was holding a hanger with something long and black on it.

Audra got up for a closer look. The sleeves were chiffon with a handful of red threads running the length. It had a thin red sash. Other details were difficult to pick out with it just hanging there. "Put it on," Audra said.

"You want me to model it for you?" There was laughter in her tone. Violet was amused by the request.

"Yes," Audra said. "I want you to put it on and come out here and, you know, twirl around and everything."

Violet laughed out loud, then she backed into her room still smiling. Audra bobbed her head to the music that now felt more like fun background noise than filler. She sang a line or two of the chorus. It only took Violet a minute to change her clothes. She stepped out of her room with a little hop. Her arms were held out from her sides in a display posture.

"Very nice!" Audra exclaimed. The dress was much improved by having a person fill it, especially a young woman as pretty as Violet. Her dark hair was pinned up the same as it was nearly every day, but the cascading curls took on a fancy look over the special occasion dress. The skirt just covered her knees and was very full. It flared out as Violet spun around. "You can't possibly say it's boring or funeral-appropriate with those pops of red."

"I know," Violet said. "I can't believe Rosie suggested this one. She's been so adamant about her wedding not taking on a Christmasy theme just because it's in December."

"Not everything red is Christmasy."

Violet laughed. "That's exactly what she said. She said red is also the color of Valentine's Day and hearts and love and it's totally appropriate for weddings. I pointed out that the dress is still mostly black. I was trying to say that it was what she wanted even though I really liked it, too. Rosie understood. She said something sarcastic like, 'I guess you'll have to put up with some dull black after all,' to give me a hard time about how I've been resisting black. But my mom missed the sarcasm. She started trying to assure me that I could choose whatever color I want when it's my wedding. It took us a minute to figure out what she was going on about. Then I don't remember how it started, but Rosie and I started asking her a bunch of questions about what she'd pick for each of us if it was up to her. It was funny to watch Mom refuse to give opinions while also trying not to grimace at our ridiculous suggestions. Rosie found this orange flowery dress she pretended was better than white and… eventually, I reminded them both that I needed to get back to work and could we just buy the dress already. Mom said, 'Wait. You like this one?'

Rosie and I laughed." Violet spun around as she finished talking and ended with a quick dance step. She clearly enjoyed being dressed up.

Audra enjoyed the story. Mostly. "So you bought this yesterday?" she asked.

Violet nodded.

"Why didn't you tell me all about it yesterday?"

"Oh." Violet stopped swaying and looked at the ground. "It's stupid." She sighed and returned her eyes to Audra. "I was just feeling a little down about the idea of... going to the wedding by myself. It didn't bother me... I mean, I hadn't even thought about it until... well, until I entertained thoughts that I might maybe have someone to take me."

That was Audra's fault, and she wanted to fix it. "You can still have someone take you even if it's not a date. I bet Alison wouldn't mind if you borrowed Trevor. Although Trevor might mind. He doesn't dance." She rolled her eyes and was about to suggest Ryan instead.

"No, it's not the same." Violet shook her head with only a little sadness. "And it really doesn't matter. I just... Besides... things might look different by December. Maybe I... I don't know." She ended with a shrug.

Audra let it go. But the conversation had drifted close enough to what neither wanted to talk about that she couldn't help thinking about it. The guilt of what she'd done was pressing on Audra to confess. What good would that do? Audra might feel unburdened, but the knowledge that Logan had kissed someone else right before he picked her up would not make Violet feel any better. Maybe Audra could offer a more generic apology. "I'm sorry I didn't discuss your feelings with Logan first" sounded very wrong. "I'm sorry I thought he'd be interested in you" sounded offensive. "I'm sorry it didn't work out" sounded empty. And possibly like she regretted failing more than she regretted that Violet was wounded by it.

"Don't say it," Violet said suddenly.

Audra wondered which version her expression had been hinting at. "What?"

"You have nothing to apologize for," Violet said. "I'm really not mad at you. I appreciate that you tried to help, and the rational side of me knows it's better in the long run that I know where I stand so I don't… it's probably better. I'm not mad. I've only been quiet because I know if we talk about it, then I'm going to ask. And I don't want to ask."

Audra almost said, "What?" She caught herself just in time. She didn't understand, but if there was something Violet didn't want to ask, she probably didn't want to spell out the question either. Instead, Audra said, "Okay. We won't talk about it."

"I better change back." Violet ducked into her room again.

The cover of the book Violet was reading caught Audra's eye. She moved to the couch and picked it up. Audra preferred fiction but tried to read at least one religious book each year. Hopefully, that was enough to ward off sloth. The last few she read had been recommendations from Violet. Audra opened to the table of contents to read the chapter titles.

"Hey, are you trying to steal my book?" Violet joked. She was dressed for bed again.

"No, just, uh… keeping it warm for you."

Violet smiled as she took it back.

"Is it any good?" Audra asked.

"So far I'm loving it." Violet tapped the bookmark sticking out the top. "But you can see I'm not very far in. Not sure I'm going to recommend it yet."

"Do you want to keep reading tonight, or do you want to play a game?"

A flicker of hope crossed her face before she turned towards the kitchen table and back. "You're not imagining masterpieces tonight?"

"No." Audra glanced at the sketchbook, too. Corn was stupid. "I'm having a dry spell."

"Sorry. I'm sure you'll get some inspiration soon."

She knew Violet was trying to be encouraging so Audra tried to look as though the words hadn't bounced off her frustration and landed in a pool of muck. She moved towards their shelf of games to find a suggestion.

"*Lost Cities*?" Violet said from behind her, then she laughed as Audra's shoulders slumped dramatically. They hadn't played that one in a while. Because Violet always won.

Audra grabbed it from the shelf anyway. "Yeah, okay." Regardless of Violet's opinion, Audra still felt she owed her. Playing a game that wasn't her first choice was a small offering.

Violet shuffled the cards while Audra flattened the board.

"Are you going to let me win this time?" Audra asked.

"I don't *always* win."

"Feels like it."

Violet didn't respond.

Audra decided to take that as agreement. "Do you remember that customer I told you about? The one who keeps watching the door?"

"Yeah." Violet was turning all her cards right side up, but she was also listening.

"She let slip today that the person she's watching for is a guy."

"The plot thickens," Violet said with a smile.

"She said it when she noticed me talking to Logan like I knew him," which was something Audra had not meant to let slip. "He was mostly there to talk to Ryan," she quickly added.

Violet nodded, but she hadn't quite hidden a flinch.

That was the boundary. Their friendship was safe as long as Audra could avoid mentioning Logan for a while. She would try harder. She focused most of her comments on the game they were playing. It was no surprise when Violet won. Audra was close though. She had enjoyed the game more than usual when she went into the last round feeling as though she had a chance. She also enjoyed that Violet was rooting against herself to prove she didn't always win.

They retired to their respective rooms on good terms. Audra got comfortable for bed, then sat cross-legged on the side of it with her prayer journal open on her lap. Before writing, she discussed with God the highlights and lowlights of her day. One of the highest highpoints surprised her. It was Fred's tip. Though it had initially thrown her, she had to admit that Ryan was right. Fred loved being generous, and Audra loved allowing him the opportunity. It had been barely a blip in her day, but reflecting back on accepting someone's generosity was the moment that made her smile most. One of the lowlights was having to admit Ryan was right.

*T*onight would be the test. After tonight, Audra would have a much better idea of how long it would be before things were completely normal between her and Violet. Audra didn't know how long she'd carried a torch for Logan so she didn't know how long she might need to get over him. But when Audra first announced her mission as matchmaker, the one thing Violet had asked was that she not make Friday nights awkward.

It was Friday, the first Friday since their relationship got rocky. If she and Violet could still drop in on the guys and act naturally, Audra could rest assured that things would continue to get smoother. But if there was tension, if Violet was uncomfortable there, then Audra would know she owed her more than time – though she didn't know what – to repair the damage.

Fortunately, there was a temporary reprieve either way. Violet was doing a better job of forgetting about her disappointment or at least hiding it while they had visitors. Alison and Elaine had already arrived by the time Audra got home from work. They were laughing with Violet while they picked up a bunch of Tichu cards from the floor.

"I don't know if I should ask what's so funny," Audra said, "or why the cards are all over the floor."

"Both," Alison said.

Audra was already starting to chuckle as the joy was contagious. And because she'd been feeling as though she needed a laugh.

Violet sat back on her heels as she grabbed the last card. "Elaine was telling us about a customer who couldn't understand why you couldn't put the drawers in upside-down without moving the guides and how she wanted to ask why anyone would even... It wasn't that funny, but I happened to laugh right when I was about to shuffle and I somehow sent the cards flying across the room. I don't think I could have arced them like that on purpose if I tried."

The laughter subsided, but they were all still smiling as they sat down to begin the game. Now that Audra's work schedule made them start later, they jumped right in. Though there was still plenty of talking and socializing while they played. Alison mentioned how much she had enjoyed the birthday dinner for Audra's dad. She came with Trevor, which their mom had thought was super sweet.

Then Audra remembered something she wanted to ask Elaine about. "Your friend Sheila came into the restaurant for lunch this week," she said.

"Oh?" Elaine's questioning eyes had evidently picked up on there being more to that observation.

"She was not alone."

"Not alone how?" Alison asked.

"She was with one of my grandpa's friends on what appeared to be a date, and of course there's nothing wrong with that, but I was surprised. After hearing her rant at Alison for dating Trevor, she's kind of the last person I would have expected to see with a man, or at least with a man and not screaming at him for, you know, existing."

Elaine chuckled at the assessment but did not comment on the shock. "I understand she's already seen Fred several times, and you can take some credit for their meeting."

"Really? How?"

"He came in our shop to check out your work while she was there."

Audra hadn't expected to be a matchmaker without knowing it, but she still felt disappointed that coincidence didn't offer the slightest compensation for her failure with Violet.

Violet wasn't thinking about that. She was apparently distracted by math. "Is he like a ton older than her? I mean, I'm not saying it matters. It's just... it seems like your mother's friend," she pointed at Alison, "and your grandfather's friend," she moved her finger towards Audra, "would be a generation apart."

Elaine nodded. "Not a whole generation, but he does have about twelve years on her. When we're talking about people over sixty... well, it's not the same as someone twelve years older than you girls."

"Yeah, but a few years would be okay if... uh..." Violet trailed off with a glance at Audra, who could hear the rejection in the unfinished sentence. Violet perked up right away with a less personal direction for the conversation. "What if you were somehow only allowed to date, and eventually marry, someone who's the same age?"

"The same age right now?" Alison said. "What if you were both, say, twenty-seven," that was Alison's age, "but one of you would turn twenty-eight a few months sooner?"

"Maybe you had to be born within six months of each other," Violet said.

"Then I'd be a lawbreaker," Elaine said. "Jim is fourteen months older than me."

"And Alison would have to say goodbye to Trevor," Audra pointed out. He was younger.

"Yeah, I meant more, um..." Violet tipped her head while she found the words. "Just hypothetically, in general, how would it change the... Would there be a lot more pressure to find someone while you're still in school, since that's the last time you're really grouped by age?"

"Maybe," Audra said.

"Or would more things focus on age?" Alison asked.

"I don't know about that," Audra said. "The places people meet like work or clubs or... They're not usually intended as matchmaking tools."

"Dating websites would have to make age the primary sort," Alison said. "But it would be a difficult rule to enforce. Marriage licenses could be refused but dating police would be..."

"I know. That was one of the more inane conversations I've started." Violet had a self-deprecating tone. "Whose turn is it?"

"I think Audra won the last trick," Elaine said.

Audra thought back, and that sounded right. She refocused on her hand to continue the game. The conversation followed who was getting better cards for a while, with a few sidetracks related to what people had done during the week. Elaine was still struggling to remember a few rules, but she and Violet pulled out a victory anyway. Audra congratulated them while she put the cards away.

"I guess we have to check on the guys now," Alison said as she pushed in her chair.

Audra smiled. She always wanted to visit the guys' game. It was nice that she wasn't always the one to suggest it.

"I'll stay here tonight," Violet said. "A few things on my to do list." She sounded nonchalant. The others simply nodded and said goodnight as they moved towards the door.

Audra knew the real reason. She knew Violet was embarrassed to go over there now that she'd revealed her interest in, and been rejected by, Logan. If only Audra could say a few magic words to make everyone friends again. But it had taken Audra almost three months to talk herself into facing Logan after he refused her. It would be hypocritical to expect much less from Violet.

Alison led the way out but let Audra go ahead when they got to her brothers' door. She walked in without knocking or ringing the bell. She greeted them in a cheerful voice so that, hopefully, the other guys wouldn't suspect anything odd about Violet staying home.

"Hey, Audra," Ryan said.

"Is our doorbell broken?" Trevor asked. "I didn't hear it."

Cameron was nodding greetings at all the women.

"Didn't ring it," Audra said. "I didn't want to give you warning to jump up and lock me out." The joke was as dead as a doornail, or a coffin nail as Dickens might say. She was trying too hard to cover the fact that she'd forgotten her usual entrance. It didn't help that Logan looked way too happy to see her.

"Violet's not with you?" Ryan asked. He was leaning back in his chair to see the door Elaine had closed behind her.

"Not tonight," Alison said.

Audra was watching Logan's face for a reaction. He'd already gone back to looking at his cards. On the one hand, if he could act naturally, that would probably help Violet do the same. On the other hand, he should be showing a bit of regret or remorse or at least sympathy after he hurt her.

There was movement out of the corner of her eye as Ryan pulled his cards close to his chest.

"I wasn't even trying to look at them," Audra snapped.

He only raised an eyebrow in reply.

He was right though. She had no reason to be upset, at least not with him. She tried to pull back her temper.

Trevor went out first and turned to Alison to confirm some weekend plans. She teased that they could spend more time together on Saturday if he'd wait until Sunday for church. Trevor hated mornings. The rest of them went to a 10 AM Mass, which wasn't even that early. But Alison had already figured out that it was fun to watch him squirm at the prospect of being fully functional before noon. Legitimate plans were made, then Alison took her mom home.

The next round finished the game. Audra had hardly been watching. It wasn't as much fun without Violet. Or maybe the silent tension she felt building between her and Logan made it less fun. Something made her want to leave before the next game started. "I guess I'll call it a night, too," she said. "But I want to talk to Logan for a minute first." She tipped her head for him to follow her as she moved towards the door.

A couple of groans sounded from behind – most likely from Ryan and Trevor – though she wasn't sure if it was because of her pulling him from the game or because he came along without protest.

Audra turned to face Logan as soon as they got to the sidewalk and knew she'd made a big mistake. It had been an impulse, a thought as she left that yelling at Logan might make her feel better about the situation. She knew it wouldn't as soon as she had a moment to finish the thought. Now that they were alone, the weird tension was worse. Remembering how he'd kissed her made Audra feel as though there was something stronger than friendship between them. As any of Jane Austen's characters would say, however, there was no such understanding. There was only the knowledge that there might have been, if only Logan hadn't waited so long.

Logan still expected her to say something, to have a reason for dragging him outside. In fact, he might know her well enough to suspect yelling at him was the reason. He widened his soft brown eyes and said, "So?"

"Nothing," Audra said. "Go back to your game." She tried to take a step.

He reached out an arm so that it blocked her path. Now Audra had three choices. She could run into the grass around his arm, like a child. She could finish her step into it and probably end up in a scary wonderful hug. Or she could stop right where she was. She froze.

Logan smiled briefly at her decision before he lowered his arm. "If you have something to say," he said, "I'm all ears."

Audra sighed. Yelling at him would be even less satisfying if he was ready to take it. "I just wish this had worked out differently."

"Differently as in a way you end up marrying me?"

Her eyes snapped up to his. "That is not funny, Bartholomew!"

"Do I sound like I'm kidding?"

No. He did not. Audra was speechless. What if she said something that he took as acceptance of what almost sounded like a proposal? That wasn't a real proposal, was it? Some sort of hysteria caused her to imagine announcing to everyone out of the blue that they were planning a wedding. People would think they'd been keeping the romantic side of their relationship secret. Aside from the fact that it sounded even more like an Austen novel, that was a terrible idea.

Audra's grandparents already seemed to think more was going on than she'd admit. Violet knew better, and Audra had to keep it that way. Violet was the reason she needed to stop letting her head fill with images of a future with Logan. She pictured him roughhousing with a pile of small children. She pictured quiet moments when they prayed together. She thought of the struggle over meals, where he joked with their friends about her trying to feed him weeds from the back yard and danced when she consented to serve beef. She pictured working together to string Christmas lights on a porch railing. It wasn't because it was only September that she forced the picture to evaporate.

"I think," she said slowly, "I think we need to pretend you didn't say that."

"Because you don't want to talk about it right now or because you don't ever want to?"

Audra almost asked if he meant she never wanted to talk about it or she never wanted to marry him. But that would be talking about it. She could hear their future children laughing as she told them that their dad had known her for years before he finally asked her out and when she turned him down, he asked her to marry him instead. Would refusing to entertain the possibility hurt Logan as badly as she was trying to avoid hurting Violet? How could she choose? If only he could promise another chance in the future, maybe Audra could think of something to say.

"You're not ready," he said. "You think I'm rushing. Let's take a smaller but still serious step. Tell me why I can't have a painting."

She shook her head at the abrupt shift to familiar territory. She could refuse as stubbornly as he could ask.

"Please." Logan's plaintive tone stopped her more than the word. "Tell me the truth. Tell me *why*."

The earnestness in his eyes said the reason mattered to him far more than she'd realized. Her defensive shell crumbled as her failure spilled out. "I can't paint what you want."

His eyes scrunched in confusion. "What do you mean?"

"I mean I can't," she said. "I've tried so many times."

"But that doesn't make any sense. Most of your paintings are awesome. I keep telling you which ones I like best, which ones I want."

"None of them are people."

"You don't paint people." He still sounded confused and now a little concerned. "You paint landscapes."

"I know," Audra said. "But when I first started, you told me I should paint people. You even told me a specific moment you wanted me to capture. I've been trying ever since."

"Really?"

He didn't remember. He'd dampened her dream with his lack of enthusiasm and issued a challenge that had stayed out of reach for years, and he didn't even remember. "You said landscapes were boring," she accused.

Logan bit the side of his lip in a wince. "I'm sorry, Audra. *If* I said that, it must have been before I saw any of your kooky landscapes. Even the ones that aren't my favorites aren't boring because I see you in them."

Audra had a difficult time summoning anger while he appeared appropriately chagrinned. The sweet words helped soften her mood as well, and a ball of fluff formed in her chest when Logan reached out and brushed his fingertips along her outer arm.

"I've tried to accept you may never be interested for a long time, but after..." Logan swallowed hard, and she could practically see their kiss replayed in his eyes. He closed them and said, "You can't take it back now."

"I don't want to," Audra said. "But it should never have happened in the first place. Goodnight, Logan." She walked around him towards her apartment, grateful that he didn't try to stop her again.

13

$\mathcal{L}$ ogan walked in slightly stunned. By the look in her eyes, he'd expected Audra to yell at him about something. But she'd relaxed immediately and appeared regretful without unloading.

"About time," Trevor said.

"These guys had nearly talked me into being the one to bring you back inside," Cameron said. "They didn't want to accidentally see anything."

The cards had been dealt while he was outside. Logan sat down and picked up his hand without commenting on the speculation that the conversation might have been going a lot better than it had. He began to sort through the cards in his hand and some of Audra's words in his head.

Had she really been trying to paint something specifically for him all this time? He was sure he'd never asked that of her. She occasionally did sketches, particularly before she got serious about oil painting. She was the only person he knew who could draw recognizable people. Had she somehow taken a compliment as a request? Or had he made on offhand suggestion that she'd taken to heart? Probably the most important question was whether or not the revelation would change anything. Would Audra forgive him for the wasted effort he hadn't asked for? Would she finally let him have a painting? Unfortunately, he'd no longer be satisfied with one of her works. He wanted all of Audra.

"Must be the guy not paying attention who has the one."

"Of course it is. I gave it to him."

The voices broke through just enough for Logan to understand they were giving him a hard time for holding up the game. He studied his hand long enough to pull out cards for the first trick. He tried to play while still wondering how he could be so close and so far from a relationship with Audra. There was no doubt that she wanted it, too. Her kiss had been raw and honest. But she'd also been clear that there would be no moving forward.

The sound of cards shuffling brought Logan back to the present. How had the cards gotten into his hands? He didn't remember finishing the round. Had he recorded the score? He tapped his phone to find out. It didn't help because he didn't remember what the score was before. Was that the second round or the third? A glance around the table showed Ryan holding out his hand. It must be his deal. Logan passed the cards and trusted that one of the guys would have said something if the score needed to be updated.

How in the world was he supposed to get past this obstacle Audra had thrown up? He could wait if he thought it was necessary. He certainly didn't want to do anything to damage Audra's friendship with Violet. That was important to her. But he was sure Audra was wrong. Whatever Violet was upset about had nothing to do with him.

Logan didn't consider himself any kind of genius at reading women, but Violet had been more interested in the door of the bowling alley than in him. She'd known he had agreed to go because Audra asked him. Something didn't make sense. The two women needed to talk to each other to figure it out. Logan got nowhere trying to talk to Audra, and he wasn't quite desperate enough to broach the subject with Violet. How could he get Audra to talk to Violet? He'd already suggested it. And he shouldn't even have to ask. They lived together, and they were women. Surely they talked.

He'd be confident he only had to give them a few days to work it out if they hadn't already proven that they worked it out incorrectly.

"Earth to Logan."

It was Cameron's voice. He wore an impatient expression.

Trevor was pretending to knock his head against the table.

Ryan sighed heavily. "This is the slowest game we have ever played." He gestured to some cards on the table.

"Uh… whose tens?" Logan asked.

Two of the guys rolled their eyes and pointed at Ryan, who also took an extended glimpse at the ceiling.

Logan nodded and mentally returned to the game. Until a thought snuck up on him. Had he just proposed to Audra!? He'd only meant to suggest they should be moving in that direction. The suggestion shouldn't have been alarming so her reaction was more understandable if she took it as something more formal. He wasn't upset that he'd asked her, or might have asked her, but that he'd done it sloppily. Audra deserved words from the heart not the spur of the moment. Maybe he'd get a chance to do it right since she'd as good as rejected him. No, actually she'd refused to even talk about it. That wasn't as good as a rejection. It was worse. She could have at least given some kind of confirmation that –

"What are you doing!?"

Logan looked up at Ryan's irritation. It was directed at Logan, who was absently shuffling the cards.

"We haven't counted those yet," Ryan said.

"Some of us aren't even out yet." Cameron waved a hand between himself and Trevor. They were each holding a few of the cards.

"Oh." Logan examined the cards in front of him. There was no way he could separate the points. He was pretty sure he'd taken at least one trick but knew nothing beyond that. He cast apologetic glances at his friends. Maybe one of them remembered who won what.

Trevor tossed his cards on the table. "Forget it," he said. "We'll have to start the round over."

"Convenient," Ryan said, "since you and Logan weren't doing well."

Trevor sighed. "There isn't much hope for us anyway since only one of us is playing."

"Man, what did Audra do to you?" Cameron groaned. His question was rhetorical.

The guys already had some idea why he was having trouble paying attention, and Logan didn't think they could be any more annoyed. With nothing much to lose, he said, "Okay, how do I win her over?"

Trevor snorted. "You want advice on dating my sister?" Then he just shook his head.

Logan turned to Cameron.

Cameron shrugged with a glance at Trevor. It wasn't clear if he had no advice to give or thought Trevor would halt the conversation if he tried.

It was unlikely that Ryan would offer any help either, but Logan looked that way just in case.

Ryan stared back for several moments. He began to redeal as he spoke. "For the sake of the game, I will say only that you probably have it easier than most of us."

"How so?"

"You know Audra's a sucker for all the stereotypical stuff. Grandma May got flowers as an early birthday present, and Audra was going on about it to at least half the customers like it was the best thing Grandpa ever did. Something pretty scores points with her every time."

"That's actually a good point," Trevor conceded. "Remember when I wanted her to talk to the landlord about me moving in here? She was reluctant until I presented her with that tube of glitter paint."

"Try not to think of it as a bribe if you get her something," Ryan said.

"The paint wasn't a bribe," Trevor said. "It was a thank you present."

"That you gave her *before* she talked to the landlord," Ryan added.

Trevor was grinning at the semantics, unless the cards he was fanning out were really good.

Logan showed his gratitude by trying harder to keep his head in the game. He wasn't sure about the idea though. It was absolutely true that Audra went gooey over anything pretty and lit up even when fictional characters got good gifts. But she probably wouldn't accept anything from him at the moment. That was kind of the problem.

What if he didn't give it to her personally? If he had something delivered, would it force her to have the conversation she needed to have with Violet? Or would she just hide it and get really, really mad? Those were questions to address *after* he lost at Tichu.

****

Ryan might have been right that Logan was luckier than some guys in at least one regard. Audra was easy to shop for. Logan had already learned that through past occasions. If he had any trouble with ideas – or waited until the day before to think about it – he could always buy her new paint or canvases. That fallback wouldn't work this time. It wasn't attention-getting, either for Audra or Violet. A package of art supplies could look like something Audra ordered for herself.

Logan wasn't worried about ideas though. He had several. He was worried about whether or not sending them was the right thing to do. Was it underhanded to hope romantic trinkets would spark a conversation? They didn't have to sit down and have a deep emotional discussion. All he needed was for Violet to say something like, "Oh, you and Logan? That's fine with me."

Beyond the Violet problem though, Logan needed to do this because when he accidentally almost proposed, Audra had thought it was a joke. Maybe if he'd sent something sooner, she wouldn't have had time to develop the misunderstanding with her roommate. Logan was done being patient. He was going to make a serious effort and either end up with Audra or go down in flames trying.

He left for work early Monday morning. Since Trevor would be next door visiting his grandparents, Logan walked into the January Café first to greet all of them.

"Now there's a sight for sore eyes," May exclaimed.

Logan waved at the perky, gray-haired woman behind the counter. He recognized the back of his friend slumped against the other side of it. Two middle-aged women were having breakfast at a small side table. They glanced up at May's voice but quickly returned to their meal. They were already ignoring the boisterous laughter from the back corner table.

Paul called out to Logan above the noise of his friends, "Howdy, stranger!"

"Good morning," Logan answered, looking between Paul and May as he approached the counter.

Paul shook his head. "That's not your line."

"It's been so long since he's been in he's probably forgotten," May said.

Logan sighed because he knew what they wanted him to say. It had been at least a month since he'd seen them so he played along. "I'm not a stranger," he said.

"Are you sure?" Paul asked. "They don't get much *stranger* than you." His buddies chuckled over the joke that never seemed to get old.

Logan slapped Trevor on the shoulder. He hadn't yet looked up from the mug of coffee he seemed to be contemplating. At the jostling, he only squinted less.

"What brings you in this morning?" May asked.

"Gotta be breakfast at this hour," Paul said.

May shot her husband a disgusted glance. "I'm giving the boy a chance to be more specific."

"Uh, actually I already ate," Logan said. "I'm just here to say hello."

"We'll see about that." May turned around and disappeared into the kitchen.

Trevor sipped his coffee before he looked at Logan. "What are you doing here?"

The gruff, unwelcoming tone was easy to ignore because it was just how Trevor sounded in the morning. "On my way to talk to Alison."

"Hmm." Trevor's forehead wrinkled in concentration. He appeared to be struggling to process the statement or form a follow-up question. "You, uh… what about?"

"I want her to make a frame for one of Audra's paintings," Logan said. "Don't mention it to Audra though." He wasn't really worried about Trevor spoiling the surprise. He was more likely to forget the conversation than to repeat it.

Trevor's mouth moved silently. He brought the mug to his lips rather than voice whatever he was still confused about. More coffee was for the best.

"See ya," Logan said. He raised a hand to Paul, but May popped through the kitchen door before he'd fully turned to leave.

"Take this with you." Her voice was soft yet commanding, suggesting that a refusal would both hurt her feelings and provoke her wrath.

Logan reached for the cinnamon muffin wrapped in a napkin. He felt immediately that it was warm. No threat was necessary for him to accept it. "With pleasure," he said. "Thanks." He took a big bite to prove he would enjoy it. The treat tasted as wonderful as it smelled, and it was halfway gone by the time he made it to the door.

Next Love's fancy door gave the impression that he was about to enter a mansion right before he entered a warehouse. Elaine Brachy smiled and waved from the side where she was chatting with a customer. Logan returned the wave before making his way towards the back. The place was stuffed with wooden furniture. They managed to keep a few feet down the center clear. Logan got partway to Alison's work corner before he spotted her sitting on the floor attacking an end table with a screwdriver. She was simply taking the handle off its drawer. It was the satisfied expression as she set the part aside that gave the impression she'd been attacking it.

Alison stood up when she saw him coming. She pushed her long brown ponytail over her shoulder as she stepped around some of her mess to greet him. "Logan," she said, "can I help you with something?" Her question was polite shopkeeper, but between the lines was a hint that she didn't expect his visit to be about the shop.

"Yeah. I know you've made frames for a few of the people who bought Audra's work." He nodded that way and let them both appreciate the paintings for a moment before continuing. "And I hoped you could make one for me."

"Oh, she gave you one?"

"Uh... not yet." Logan was optimistic that he'd be able to get one soon, and when he already had a frame for it, Audra would believe he wanted it. "But you don't need the painting since they're all the same size, right?"

"Not really." Alison tipped her head as she considered. "It can be nice to make sure the stain doesn't clash, but I could use something neutral. Or did you have natural wood in mind?"

"I don't have anything in mind."

"Hmm. That either makes my job a lot easier or a lot harder."

"I'd like a fairly simple frame that could go around any of these paintings." He swept an arm towards them. "But that doesn't look like it could go with any old painting."

Alison narrowed her eyes at him. "Harder," she said.

"No, I just mean, can you do something to it so it isn't just a square?"

"It'll be a rectangle." Alison seemed to be trying not to laugh at his inept descriptions.

Logan thought about what he was trying to say. "Can you carve a design or put notches in the edges or something so it isn't a flat piece of wood?"

"Oh... I think I might get it." She smiled and nodded. "Something to make it a little special but not too elaborate."

"Exactly," Logan said. This was why she was the professional. When she said something vague, it made sense. They talked about price and how long it might be before it was ready. Alison assured him she would avoid mentioning it to Audra without being asked. He trusted her word and her ability. He walked out along the side wall rather than the center so he could admire the art more closely. Something was missing though.

The snowy forest one that he liked was no longer hanging among the others. Audra had evidently sold it to someone else after refusing him. That stung. But at least he wouldn't have trouble finding another one he liked. Several were already sound candidates.

14

*A*udra was mixing muffin batter and enjoying the exertion of beating it. The lunch customers hadn't begun to fill the restaurant. Ryan was out front doing a couple of job interviews. Audra was picking up some slack in the kitchen. It wasn't the unnecessary reminder that Ryan was in charge that was making her cranky though. It was the flowers.

And the stuffed puppy.

And the fruit.

And the sweet notes that came with each.

Mostly, it was Logan.

She took a deep breath to steady her arm before she added the blueberries. No need to crush those just because Bartholomew Fuller was being annoying. She folded the fresh berries into the batter and began to spoon it into the pan. Ben, a first-year college student, was preparing chocolate chip muffins on the other side of the table. He was a few steps behind Audra but so far had not touched his phone or done anything else wrong. Unfortunately, that left her mind free to dwell on all the things Logan had done wrong.

The flowers arrived on Monday, a beautiful bunch of white carnations with red, pink and blue tips on the petals. Audra loved them. They made her think of a brand-new paintbrush dipped into paint for the first time. Logan knew that. He knew they were her favorites. The note that came with them said, "I know these are your favorite flowers."

Audra had been lucky. The flowers arrived in the morning window after Violet had left for work and before Audra did. The two of them had gone the whole weekend without reminders of the matchmaking failure. The last thing they needed was a romantic gesture aimed at Audra to reignite the friction. She'd enjoyed the carnations for a few minutes, drinking in their lovely scent, before she took them to the dumpster outside.

Tuesday's gift was more difficult to hide. A package arrived while both women were at work. Violet had brought it inside and left it on the table for Audra. Since she hadn't ordered anything and since she had gotten something she hadn't ordered the previous day, Audra took the little box into her room to open. She pulled out a stuffed dog that fit perfectly on her palm. It gazed up at her with deep brown eyes under slightly lowered lids and had the smoothest velvety soft ears ever. She would have been happy to nuzzle it against her cheek or set its cuteness on a shelf. Instead, it was crammed into the bottom of a box.

Violet had asked about the package later, just casually asked if it'd been anything good. Audra told her it was nothing important, which it wasn't. It was a small, inexpensive trinket. But she'd felt as though she was hiding something important when she wasn't more specific. Violet could tell. She'd given Audra a funny look, but then quickly moved on. Logan was very lucky that it hadn't brought back the tension between the friends.

He was pushing his luck on Wednesday. A cooler of fruit arrived in the evening. Violet had answered the door and signed for it. Then she announced that the box was addressed to Audra and held it out to her expectantly. Trying to hide it at that point would have been entirely too suspicious, not to mention impossible.

Audra tore into it hoping she could somehow pass off whatever was inside as a friendly gesture. The fruit was cut into geometric shapes, arranged on a stack of plates in different patterns. It was pretty but not overtly romantic. Audra didn't remember anyone ever sighing over a box of fruit, though she had been feeling a bit of relief.

There was a tiny envelope inside with a note that said, "I finally figured out what's missing from your diet. You need more fruit." She could hear the sarcasm in his words, and it made her laugh. She shared what it said with Violet, and she laughed at the joke, too. They put the fruit away without further comment. Audra thought they'd dodged another bullet.

There were two things bothering her that morning. Three if she counted Logan. He'd been bothering her all week. But one of Audra's concerns arose that morning. She and Violet had shared one of those plates of fruit over breakfast. They hadn't talked about where it came from, but Violet seemed overly happy about it, even offering a knowing smile as she stabbed her fork into a piece of pineapple. It was that moment when Audra realized she had said Logan thinks *we* don't eat enough fruit. What if, by including Violet, she'd unwittingly given her false hope that Logan was forming some interest in her? That wasn't any kinder than letting her see gifts intended for someone else.

The other worry was that some other even more difficult to hide surprise was going to show up today to continue the trend. Logan was being so stupid. Audra had already told him they couldn't form that kind of relationship while Violet was vulnerable. How could he possibly not realize that Violet would see the gifts he was sending?

Audra's hand froze with the spoon over the cup she'd just filled. Logan wasn't stupid. He knew exactly what he was doing. He *wanted* Violet to see the gifts. He evidently believed Violet would give permission, and that would clear his path. But just because Violet wouldn't stand in their way didn't mean she'd feel good about it. It wouldn't stop Audra from hurting her friend. Logan's timing was dreadful. Audra frowned and finished scraping out her bowl. When she set it in the sink, it clunked as loudly as if she'd dropped it. She needed to relax.

But she also needed to take back her thought that Logan wasn't being stupid. It was typical guy behavior to think action would fix what only time could fix. She was mad at him for that. And mad at him for sending flowers she had to throw away. They had been so pretty. She'd cringed when she heard the truck coming to empty the dumpster. If she hadn't been sure they'd already been squished by someone else's trash, she might have been tempted to run outside for one last look at those beautiful carnations.

"Muffins are already in the oven?" Ryan asked as he entered the kitchen. It wasn't really a question but relief at the obvious. "Thanks, Audra. That second interview took way longer than it should have. She could talk forever about nothing and cannot take a hint when it's time to stop. She'd never let the customers eat in peace. I had to straight up tell her the interview was over and she had to get out because I had work to do. I'd already thanked her for her time twice."

Audra raised an eyebrow at the declaration.

"Well, I hope I said it nicer than that," Ryan said. "I hired the first one though. She'll start Monday."

"Did you tell her you weren't going to hire her?"

Ryan looked confused, and also distracted. He was looking at the employee who was staring at the sink as though he'd forgotten how to use it. "Oh, the... I said we'd be in touch if we had a spot for her so she'll figure it out eventually." He rolled his eyes before he moved away but began giving instructions in a very patient tone.

Audra returned to the dining room to await customers. It was only a few minutes before she was able to welcome the start of the lunch crowd, a pair of women who worked in the office at the high school. They wanted about a dozen sandwiches to take back with them. Audra had to consult with Ryan because the January Café hadn't done to go orders when she last worked there and still did very few. This was the first one she'd prepared that had food for more than one person. She didn't know the expected packaging. She told the women as they claimed the bags that they could call ahead to have it ready next time. But based on the way they'd sat huddled in conversation, she suspected they didn't mind an excuse to wait.

The restaurant filled up fast. Fortunately, the two employees who were running late entered near the front of the crowd. That freed Audra to chat with Katie while she was there. She planned to invite her to join that Friday's card game. She'd been building up to it during the week. She'd even told her about the flowers. Sort of. Some of the details were left out so as not to violate Violet's privacy. She'd only explained that a guy had sent her flowers with poor timing when he *knew* the timing was bad.

Katie had guessed it had been the guy she'd seen Audra talking to. And she'd sympathized at not being able to enjoy the pretty flowers. Audra felt that they'd shared enough – though Katie still hadn't given any details on her mystery man, she'd said she might need Audra's help if he ever came in – that an invitation would not be out of place. Audra felt a little silly about working up her courage for it, yet nervous about rejection all the same.

Katie closed her book and shoved it aside as Audra set her typical lunch in front of her.

"So Katie," Audra started, "I'm wondering if, um… Have you ever heard of Tichu?"

She shook her head. "No, is that a food?"

Audra laughed self-consciously. "That's a good guess because I asked while…" She cleared her throat. "I get together with a few friends on Friday nights to play a game called Tichu. It's a card game, but it doesn't use a normal deck. You take tricks like Hearts or Spades, but…"

"Wait. How do you spell Tichu?" Katie suddenly seemed very interested.

"T-I-C-H-U."

"Oh!" Katie nodded and waved her hand around. "I *have* heard of that. I just didn't know, apparently, how to pronounce it. I've only seen it in print."

Audra didn't ask where she'd seen it. She wanted to plow ahead while she had Katie's eager attention. "Well, one of the women I play with, she wants us to replace her because she says we stay up too late. I mean, we're usually done by like 9:30 or so, but she's a little older and… Anyway, would you like to play? Do you know how?"

"I don't," Katie said. "I'd be very interested in learning, but… Do you want to play with someone who doesn't know what she's doing?"

"Sure. One of the others – Alison is her name – hasn't been playing very long either. It's a casual game."

"Great. Yeah. Count me in. You said Fridays, right?"

"Can you come tomorrow?"

Katie nodded, still looking eager. They arranged some details with Katie writing her number on a napkin. Audra flashed back to childhood. She remembered Grandpa Paul complimenting her artistic talent after she'd drawn silly pictures on napkins at that very table.

She smiled to herself at the memory and the new plan as she returned to the kitchen. The smile faded as she pulled out her phone to text Alison that she found a new fourth for Tichu. She made sure to tell her that her mom was still welcome to watch. There was a touch of guilt at cutting out the older woman even though it was what she wanted.

The rest of the day was fairly busy. By the time Audra finished her shift, she'd almost forgotten to be mad at Logan. That must have been the reason for a moment of excitement at the thought that there might be another surprise from him. She tamped it down. If there was a gift, she and Violet might have to talk about it. But that didn't mean Audra had to admit anything hurtful. She could be strong and focus on their friendship and not on the thing she did wrong that Violet didn't need to know.

Violet seemed happy when Audra came in. There was music playing, and she was singing along. "Hi," Audra said.

Violet waved, then turned down the music. "You ate at work, right?"

Audra nodded, though it seemed a strange question. They both knew she preferred the food at her grandparents' place to that at Mackenzie's and had been eating there since her schedule changed. It was a nice perk. Why would today be different? She went into her room to drop off her bag and take off her shoes. The music was gone and so was Violet when she returned to the living room.

There was junk mail on the counter. She and Violet always saved mail addressed to the other even when it was clearly nothing more than ads. There was a pang of disappointment before she reminded herself that she didn't *want* to find anything from Logan. Movement drew her attention to where Violet was now standing in her doorway, sort of half in and half out. She seemed to be holding something out of sight.

"Are you, um…" Audra sent her a quizzical look. "What are you doing?"

"I'm hiding something," Violet said, "until you're comfortable. Are you comfortable?"

Something weird was going on. Audra kept her face showing her confusion. "Should I sit down?"

A smile twitched on Violet's lips before she squelched it. Then she nodded.

It did not appear that Violet was about to deliver bad news so Audra took her favorite seat on the end of the couch, leaned against the arm with her feet tucked to the other side, and said, "Okay. I'm comfortable."

"Good. We have to talk." Violet moved into the room. In the hand that had been hidden, she was carrying a bunch of helium balloons. Three were silver with purple and white confetti. One on a longer ribbon, sticking out the top, had the words "I love you" in bold letters. "Someone left this outside the front door."

Audra blinked at the display as Violet set the foil-covered weight on the coffee table. The balloons swayed in the silence. Part of Audra wanted to gasp at how sweet and pretty they were. There was enough annoyance at how inappropriate they also were to check that impulse. Did Violet know who they were from as well as Audra did? "Someone?" Audra asked.

"I haven't read the card because it has your name on it, but I think Logan is a pretty safe guess," Violet said. "They were outside when I got home so I don't know if he actually dropped them off or had them delivered."

"Oh." Audra's eyes dropped to the tiny card tied to the base of the balloons. It did in fact have her name on it, but she made no move to reach for it. She didn't know how this conversation should go and wanted to do everything she could to let Violet lead.

"I'm confused," Violet said. "I… I want to help if I can."

Audra looked up. Now she was confused.

"When we talked about Logan just a few weeks ago, you said there was only friendship between you. You said he was the one who decided that."

Audra winced at how awful this looked. She'd convinced her friend that the way was clear for her to try a relationship with Logan, and now he was sending romantic gifts to Audra. How could she explain that she hadn't encouraged him when she really had? How could she insist that she'd told him nothing could happen without admitting why that was necessary?

"I suspect he also sent you flowers this week because Mrs. Robbins asked if one of us was having some sort of lovers' quarrel. She said she saw fresh flowers tossed in the outside bin. I didn't know what she was talking about until the fruit and the mysterious package you hid in your room and…" Violet reached out and tugged the string of the highest balloon. "There aren't a lot of mixed messages here so I wonder what I'm missing."

"Nothing," Audra said. Violet had noticed absolutely everything and could probably stand to be a little less observant.

Violet tilted her head and appeared to be considering her words. She finally sat down and leveled Audra with a compassionate expression. "I honestly don't want to pry. It's just that you seem unhappy about all this." She waved her arm at the balloons. "Logan is a great guy, and you seem happier when he's around. From where I'm sitting, you two would be an awesome couple. I don't understand why it isn't happening."

It was Audra's turn to measure her words carefully. She didn't want to accuse Violet of standing in the way. Was Violet really so selfless that she didn't even see how Audra was trying to spare her feelings? "I… It just doesn't seem right to… after how terribly I failed at my matchmaking mission."

Violet's eyes widened in surprise, and she even sat back a bit. "You… you're worried about being happy with Logan because I don't have any prospects?"

"Well, it's… I wouldn't…" Audra was stumbling over which thought to voice first. She wanted to contradict the idea that Violet didn't have prospects. That sounded as though her romantic life was hopeless when she was a smart, beautiful woman who should be far from hopeless. And it also sounded as though the failure with Logan had been her fault. It was Audra's fault. She wanted to apologize for ever thinking it was a good idea to try to play matchmaker.

"My very single status should have no bearing on…" Violet stopped and bit her lip. "Okay. Hold on. If we're going to go here, you might as well tell me how bad it was. What exactly did he say?"

"What did who say?"

"Ryan."

"Ryan?" Audra found another layer of confusion. Why were they talking about Ryan all of a sudden?

"I've spent too much energy trying not to ask. I assume he refused because he figured out the plan," Violet said. "Was he that horrified at being fixed up with me? Or did he try to sound like it was a bad time or something generic? I suppose the new job could almost... sort of... maybe count as an excuse. I suppose if he was just surprised..." Violet was rambling about something that didn't make any sense, yet she seemed to expect Audra to have an answer.

Audra just continued to attempt to grind the details into something coherent.

"I think I can take it," Violet said. "I'm probably imagining worse."

All the words, together with Violet's posture, revealed an important part of the story. Audra felt the lightbulb turn on. "You like Ryan!?"

Violet stared back as though she was surprised at the surprise. "You know that."

"I..." Audra did not know that. But now that she did, wheels were turning and pieces were shifting. She needed Violet to help her figure out where to put them. "So when I... What did you think was my matchmaking plan?"

"You had Logan take me to the bowling alley so that you and Ryan could just happen to run into us there. We could pretend it wasn't a double date but still hope it felt that way. I wasn't sure how you were going to convince Ryan if he wasn't immediately sold on a spontaneous bowling trip. I was afraid you'd have to reveal something, which was why he ended up not playing along and..." Violet's expression changed as something occurred to her. "Was that not your plan?"

Audra shook her head. "I never tried to get Ryan to the bowling alley."

"Really!? So Ryan doesn't know… He doesn't know that I…"" She trailed off and pointed sheepishly at herself.

"Not from me," Audra said.

Violet nodded and fidgeted with the information. She pulled a clip out of her hair and let dark spirals pile onto her shoulders. She wadded her hair and clipped it a bit tighter than before. "Wait a minute," she said suddenly. "What *was* your plan?"

"I, um…" This was getting awkward in a way much different than Audra had predicted. She was about to admit an embarrassing mistake before she could even figure out how she'd made it. "I thought you liked Logan."

"What?" Violet laughed in surprise but quickly sobered up. "Not that there's anything wrong with him. He's nice and definitely nice-looking and… I might have developed some hopes there if it hadn't been immediately obvious that you two were meant to be together."

"That was immediately obvious to you?" Audra was skeptical. She wasn't sure it was obvious to Logan yet.

"Pretty soon anyway," Violet said. She reached out and yanked the card off the balloons and tossed it to Audra. "Which brings us back to what we should be talking about."

Audra turned the envelope over in her hands. Despite the revelation that Violet wouldn't be jealous, she still felt an impulse to reject whatever was on the card.

"Oh, my goodness!" Violet's hand flew up to her face. She peeked at Audra through her fingers. "Does Logan think that I wanted you to fix me up with him?"

"No," Audra said. The single word packed a surprising amount of petulance. Logan had been right all along. Maybe he should be the one to take up matchmaking. He could certainly give pointers on getting someone's attention. The silver balloons danced to some unseen current in the room and reflected light from a window so that it mirrored the dance on the wall and ceiling. Audra felt surrounded by the words printed in front of her. She wanted to call Logan that very second and thank him for all the annoying presents. She wanted to tell him that she loved him, too, in spite of his efforts. But something was holding her back. And it wasn't only the fact that Violet was still talking to her.

"Are you sure?" Violet asked. "Because I thought he was in on the plan. I thought he knew he was taking me to the bowling alley so you and Ryan could meet us there. What did you tell him?"

"I… Well, you were there," Audra said. "I just said he should take you bowling."

"Yeah. And of course he agreed just because *you* asked him." Violet smiled, looking mildly disgusted at how easy it had been. "But I assume you talked to him at some other time. What did you tell him after Ryan didn't show up? Do I have to be weird around him now?"

"Do you need a reason to be weird?" Audra teased.

Violet laughed through a glare. It lightened the moment, but she continued to wait for a real answer.

"Okay. I tried to convince him that you thought it was a date with him, and he insisted I didn't know what I was talking about. So you're not the one who needs to be embarrassed."

"Hmm." Violet visibly relaxed as she thought about that. "I still hate the idea that I was coming between you, but at least that's resolved now, right? I mean, you can at least open the card."

Audra stopped fiddling with the little envelope and unsealed the flap. She recognized Logan's handwriting, possible evidence that he had dropped it off himself. It said, "Tichu tomorrow night. I want to see you after." The words were not poetry. Something about the note made her feel as though she was being summoned to the principal's office. It made her smile because she could picture Logan expecting her to think that as he wrote it. "Logan wants to talk after Tichu tomorrow," she said.

"It's good we talked now then." Violet bounced to the edge

of the couch and rubbed her hands together. "With everything all straightened out, and I don't even know how you got the idea that I was interested in Logan, but now you guys can talk and… I'll be helping you plan your wedding next. I bet it won't be long. And it'll be more fun than Rosie's. I mean, I love my sister, but we have such different tastes. She thinks she's making the reception solemn, and I think she's making it stuffy and boring. I told you there's not going to be music, right?"

Audra was having trouble keeping up with the excitement of Violet's mile-a-minute speech. As long as her best friend's feelings were at stake, she didn't have to look too closely at her own feelings. Now, though, she wasn't sure what she felt.

Violet picked up on the doubt. The question about her sister seemed to drop from the air as she stopped bouncing and regarded Audra with concern. "Is something wrong?"

"Maybe," Audra said. Her natural inclination for privacy was being pushed aside by a need for advice. "I'm going to tell you what happened so you can tell me if something's wrong."

"Okay."

Audra felt better about her decision to share when Violet looked prepared to listen objectively and not as though she was about to hear a juicy piece of gossip. "Remember when Trevor and Ryan dropped me from the Tichu game?"

"Of course," Violet said. "You were really upset and rightly so. It was only a few weeks after Trevor moved into the house and you were thrilled about getting to walk to the games and then… Sorry, Cameron's taking your place."

Audra nodded. "I get it now. Sort of. I mean, I know they wanted to include Cameron, have a little guy time without their sister always there. Now that we have our own ladies' night, we can include you, too, and it's working out well. I might have even stepped aside if they had asked me. But it hurt that no one asked."

"I am glad I get to play," Violet said. Her tone still carried plenty of sympathy for the initial rejection.

"It was the very next Saturday that Logan texted me asking if he could come over for a bit."

"I remember that, too," Violet said. "You went outside to talk to him for a long time, and I hoped he was going to cheer you up."

Audra shook her head. She hadn't actually talked to Logan very long that day. She'd stayed outside after he left to try to hide that she was more upset than before. "First, he wanted to make sure I knew that Trevor hadn't told him they kicked me out. He didn't know anything about it until Cameron was already there, and then obviously, it was too late."

"Right. He couldn't make a big deal in front of Cameron." Violet was clearly following the story so far.

"That was kind of good except that I hadn't blamed him anyway. I was pretty sure it was Trevor more than Ryan, possibly even a decision he made before he had coffee."

Violet smiled.

Audra did, too. She was pleased that she could honestly joke about it. She'd truly forgiven him. "But then Logan tried to suggest that because he wasn't going to see me regularly on Fridays anymore that maybe we could establish some other thing and... I don't remember exactly how he worded it, but it felt like a pity invitation, like maybe since I couldn't play Tichu I could do something else. I said I... He had ended with the phrase 'the two of us.' I remember that for sure. That's why I asked, I said, 'But there's never going to be an us, is there?' I practically begged him to tell me he wanted an us, that I wasn't imagining all the sparks, that he... I put everything out there, and you know what he said?"

Violet shook her head, though she could tell the question was rhetorical. She was trying to shorten the pause.

"He said, 'This was a bad idea,' and left. He just walked away."

"Huh." Violet looked about as dumbfounded as Audra had felt.

"He must have panicked when he realized that asking me to do something alone might be leading me on as Grandma May would say. I was so humiliated that... Well, that's part of the reason it took me months to start checking in on the new all-guy Tichu games. And anyway," Audra gestured to the balloons, "now that he seems to have changed his mind about me, I can't tell if I'm worried he's going to change it back or if I just want to punish him because he hurt me."

"Huh," Violet said again. She pinched her lips in a thoughtful expression while she turned the story over in her mind. After a minute, she said, "Are you sure that's what happened?"

"What? Of course I'm sure." Audra gaped at her friend. She had expected an answer with a little more sympathy and a lot less question.

"It's just that... I don't believe *this* is a new thing." She pointed once again to the balloons hovering nearby almost as though Logan was in the room. "For at least as long as I've known him, he's always paid more attention to you than anyone else in the room. That's why, as I said, I never... Is there a chance you misunderstood something he said because you were upset with Trevor?"

"He's the one who walked away," Audra said.

"Did it sound like you were upset with him and wanting him to leave?" Violet asked. "What exactly did you say?"

Audra shrugged. "I'm not sure I remember my exact words."

"Well, if you don't remember, then maybe you're remembering wrong."

"I remember enough," Audra insisted. "I know I used the word *us* with all the romantic implications and he... didn't want that."

"I still think..." Violet stopped to laugh at the playfully threatening glare Audra was giving her. "Ask Logan," she said. "He wants to talk so make him tell you how he remembers that conversation. Let him know it hurt you, and that he might have to

145

do more than send balloons to make it up. And if his version sounds different, you have to come back and admit I was right."

Audra found herself smiling at the face of premature gloating. Because even though she didn't think it was possible, she still liked the idea that it hadn't happened the way she remembered.

15

*A*udra didn't exactly chase the last customers out, but it was close. Usually, if she started putting up chairs to mop the floor, anyone still hanging around would get the hint that the restaurant was closing. That Friday, only one table wasn't empty. The teenagers at it seemed oblivious to their surroundings. The way they all stared at their phones made them seem oblivious to each other, too. They were kind of loud with the laughing and exclamations and the fact that there was clearly more talking than listening going on.

The wheels of the mop bucket rumbled on the floor as Audra brought it to the dining room. She parked it by a corner and approached the stragglers. "Hey, guys. It's after seven. We're trying to close up."

She got some form of huh or what from three of the four kids. One girl actually looked up. "Oh, she's kicking us out," she said.

The kids grabbed their stuff and moved towards the door pretty quickly once they knew they should. Audra stood by ready to lock up after them. One boy was typing something as he left and banged an arm against the door frame. The last thing Audra heard before turning the lock was another boy laughing as he told him to watch where he was going. It looked like he threw a light punch against the same arm to emphasize his point.

Audra was simply relieved they were gone so she could hurry through the mopping, her final task. She wanted to get home before Katie arrived. Alison had let her know that her mom left work early with a headache so it was a perfect time to introduce the replacement player. Audra went to the back to hang up her apron and collect her bag.

Ryan was sitting in the office. Everyone else had left, and he didn't seem particularly busy. He was moving papers around on the desk as though he had all the time in the world.

"Don't you want to get home for Tichu?" she asked.

"I gotta wait for that late delivery."

"Oh, is he still not here?"

Ryan shook his head as he checked the time.

Audra had only popped in to say goodnight. Now she hesitated, wondering if she should offer to wait with him. Her presence wouldn't bring the truck any faster though.

Perhaps sensing the unspoken offer, Ryan made a shooing motion with his hand. "Don't worry, Trevor can entertain the guys until I get there."

Audra nodded and waved. She nearly ran out the door and jumped in her car feeling grateful that it wasn't her job to wait. The thought hit her that she'd been grateful other times as well, when she didn't want to repeatedly correct employees for making the same mistakes, when chopping vegetables was more fun than tallying receipts, whenever she wasn't feeling resentful that she deserved the job as much as Ryan. It was not a pleasant epiphany so she chose not to dwell on it as she made the short drive home.

A car she did not recognize was parked near her house. Katie got out of it as Audra got out of hers. Katie had not taken the closest spot. Audra waved and stopped on the sidewalk to wait for her to catch up. "Hi," she said. "You haven't been waiting long, have you?"

"No. Just a few minutes. I think your other friend just got here." She nodded towards the house.

Audra had recognized Alison's truck. "Great. We'll be able to start teaching you right away."

"I almost drove right past," Katie said. "Since your address included an apartment number, I was looking for something more, um... less mansiony."

"Yeah, it's a cool old house even if I only get one corner of it. It used to be all one house, but... well, that was a long time ago." Audra stuck her key in the lock and led Katie into her corner of the house. Alison and Violet jumped up from the couch as they entered.

Katie smiled at them and looked to Audra for introductions.

"Okay, everyone, this is Katie. That's Violet. She's the one who lives here. That's Alison. She's dating my brother."

There was some nodding and greeting. Audra dropped her bag in her room and showed Katie where she could put hers.

"We know you're a January Café fan," Violet said.

Katie nodded. "Definitely. I think I'd be eating there all the time even if..." She trailed off, possibly wondering if Audra had talked about her obsession with the door or if she'd be opening a can of worms by mentioning it.

While Audra did hope to address that topic, she didn't want to pounce on it first thing. "Where do you work?" she asked instead. "It must be close to make us a convenient lunch stop."

"Yeah." Katie appeared relieved by the less personal topic. "It's a place called EJ Industries. I do accounts payable."

"I've heard of that," Audra said, though she couldn't remember where she'd heard of it.

"It's on 105, about halfway between here and Andauk."

Audra didn't go that way often, but it was possible she was thinking of driving past it.

"Accounts payable?" Alison said. "You pay bills all day?"

"Something like that."

"Do you like it?" Violet asked. She handled some financial tasks at her job and might have similar duties to talk about with Katie.

Katie shrugged. "I spend a little too much time chasing down coworkers, but otherwise it's not bad."

"What do you mean?" Audra said. She held up a red deck of cards and motioned for everyone to move towards the table as they talked.

"Well, every invoice I pay out has to be matched to something that someone else has billed to a customer. A few people don't keep awesome records, and…" Katie ended the sentence with an eyeroll.

The other women nodded sympathetically and took seats around the table. Audra was across from Katie. The first thing she explained was that they would be partners against Violet and Alison. She fanned the cards on the table to begin the rules. When she explained the special cards, she held up the dog and said, "There are times it's okay to give your partner the dog, but for now just don't, okay?"

Alison bit back a smile because she knew her mom drove Audra nuts with her failure to remember that she didn't want it.

"Got it." Katie nodded and was clearly paying close attention. She asked questions and seemed genuinely eager to learn. Her diligence paid off as the game went fairly smoothly. There were a few rule clarifications and sometimes a hand was slow to start because they were getting to know each other between rounds. No one minded those types of pauses.

Alison and Violet won, but it seemed more due to better cards than better skills. And Katie said she had fun.

Audra stood up and stretched. "Now for part two of the evening. We go bother the guys."

"Bother the guys?" Katie was the only one still sitting, though fortunately she seemed more confused than worried or reluctant.

"I told you my brothers live next door, right?"

Katie nodded, slowly rising from her chair.

"They have their own Tichu game, and we like to end ours by seeing how they're doing," Audra said. "Alison likes the excuse to say hello to Trevor and Violet... uh, Violet and I like to say hello, too. And tonight, I'm excited to introduce you. Though you sort of met Ryan at the restaurant."

"Yeah, I... well, I've seen him anyway."

"Great. Let's go." Audra met eyes with Violet for a moment. She looked happy to come along this week and happy that Audra hadn't given a more specific reason.

The other women left ahead of Audra but intentionally dawdled to let her pass and reach the apartment door first. She rang the bell four times and smiled as she led the others inside.

****

The doorbell was a welcome sound to Logan even if he didn't need to hear it four times. Audra breezed into the room and softened the harsh ringing with her presence. He was anxious to find out if she'd settled the miscommunication regarding Violet. While he knew that couldn't happen until they were alone, the fact that Violet was right behind her was a sign they were still getting along after his gifts. That much was good to see.

Alison came in as well, but the woman behind her was not her mom.

"Hi, Alison," Trevor said.

Audra turned towards the new person as though about to explain the difference.

"Oh! Hi, Cameron," the stranger said first.

"Katherine?" he said. "Hi."

Surprised and curious glances passed around the room for a few seconds. Audra began talking slowly. "Well... *I* know K-Katherine from the January Café. She's become my favorite customer so I invited her to play Tichu. How do you know her?" She pointed at Cameron.

"From work," he said.

"Oh, that's why it sounded familiar when you told me…" Audra interrupted herself with a gasp. "What have you guys done?" She stepped quickly towards her painting, pulled out her level and grabbed each of the lower corners.

Logan wasn't sure it had moved at all when she stepped back with a satisfied expression.

"What did you think of the game?" Ryan asked Katherine. "Will you be back next week?"

"Of course she will," Audra said.

"Tichu is awesome," Trevor said. "How could she not like it?"

Katherine smiled. "I guess there's only one way to answer that."

"I bet Violet was a good teacher," Ryan said.

"*I* taught her," Audra said. "And who do you think taught Violet?"

"I believe that was me. Remember? You needed me and Trevor to come over and help you?"

"We needed four to practice. I had already taught her." Audra glared at the back of Ryan's head for a moment before she added, "By the way, how long did you have to wait for that delivery?"

"Only about fifteen minutes after you left."

"Good." She walked around the table and picked up Logan's phone. He was surprised it had taken her so long. "Hey," she said, "you guys are way ahead."

"I thought we were about to win," Ryan said. "But now I'm not sure we're even going to play." He looked pointedly at Logan.

Logan moved his attention from Audra's hands to what had happened just before she came in. He'd won the first trick so it was his lead.

"Wow." Katherine leaned forward and ran her hand along the corner of the table. She'd apparently noticed the Tichu suits on the edge. "You have a custom table?"

Trevor nodded proudly to the woman resting her hand on his shoulder. "Alison made it."

"I didn't make it," she said. "I just refinished it."

"It's amazing," Katherine said.

"Thank you." Alison and Trevor accepted the compliment together.

The game kept going while the table was admired and Ryan was quickly the last one out. Logan had gotten enough points by himself though. Audra pronounced them the winners as she entered the score for him.

"Are you going to play again?" she asked.

"Plenty of time," Cameron said.

Logan did want to play again, but he didn't want to wait through another game before he talked to Audra. And he didn't think the guys wanted to play with him distracted. "Good idea," he said. "Let me just walk the ladies out first."

"You're getting rid of us?" Alison teased.

He hoped she was teasing at least. He was preoccupied with trying to get outside with Audra. There were too many people in the room. "You usually only stay a minute, but you don't have to leave if you're not ready."

Alison laughed at his attempt to backtrack. "I'm kidding," she said. "We did only stop in to say hello." She bent forward and spoke more softly to Trevor. "I'll see you tomorrow."

All the people in the room were suddenly blocking the door. Audra was standing next to Logan, but she couldn't head outside because Trevor had stood up to give Alison a quick goodbye kiss. Katherine and Violet were closest to the door, looking at each other as though they didn't know it was time to open it. Even Ryan was standing for some reason. Why had Ryan gotten up?

Only Cameron was still in his chair. He was eyeing the crowd warily. When he looked at Logan, he said, "Try not to take a half hour this time."

Logan nodded. Assuming they were the right words, he and Audra only needed a few of them.

"Hey, um, Violet could play for Logan until he gets back," Ryan suggested.

Trevor had gotten out of the way, but now Violet stopped the movement towards the door as she turned to Logan for his permission.

"Sure," he said.

The quick answer did not speed up the exit as Katherine had to move to let Violet back around to Logan's vacated seat. Finally, the door opened. Katherine and Alison made it outside first, but they faced Audra rather than move directly to their cars.

"This really was fun," Katherine said. "We're on for the same time next week?"

Audra nodded eagerly. "And we'll talk before then about, um…" She gestured over her shoulder.

"I think we have to." Katherine's eyes were wide with meaning Logan didn't understand. He only cared that she was backing away as she spoke. "Nice to meet you, Logan."

He nodded that the feeling was mutual, waved to Alison, tried not to look too much like he was glad to be rid of either of them. Then he started to ask Audra if she was ready to start talking about the future.

She whirled on him before he got any words out, her hands animated and her expression fierce. "You made me throw away extremely beautiful flowers!"

That was not an answer. It sounded as though she liked the flowers but threw them away but was angry about… It was not an answer. "Did you talk to Violet?" he asked.

"Yes!" She yelled the definitive word that still didn't tell him what he wanted to know.

"And?" he prompted.

Her hands fell to her sides as her eyes dropped to the ground.

Her lids revealed the light blue irises tentatively. "I have to admit for her sake that you were right. She is not interested in you and did not think the bowling trip was a date. With you."

The way she tacked on the last two words was odd but unimportant. "What about you?" he asked. "Do you have interest?" He reached for her hand.

Audra let him entwine their fingers, but her grip was limp. After a few moments, she pulled away, putting her hand on her hip. "We need to talk about something first."

"Okay." First was not instead. And it wasn't no.

She stared intermittently at Logan, at his shirt, at the house behind them. It wasn't clear if she was thinking about what to say or waiting for him to say something when he had no idea what she needed to talk about.

"What is it?" he asked.

"I don't..." She inhaled sharply. "Do you remember when... when Cameron joined the game and you came over to explain, sort of, that it wasn't your idea?"

"Yes." It was a painful memory so it left a permanent impression.

"Why didn't... why didn't you... Did you realize how it would sound when you asked me to have a regular time for just the two of us?" She sounded almost as puzzled by her words as he was.

"It should have sounded like I wanted to be a significant part of your life," Logan said. "How did..." She could not possibly have interpreted it any other way, and yet there was a hint of surprise in her expression before she blew her top.

"Then why didn't you correct me!?"

"What?"

She only waited expectantly.

He searched his brain for how to answer her question, but it was only the last line of that old conversation that kept repeating in his head. "You told me there would never be an us, and you sounded really upset that I even suggested it. Are you saying you *wanted* me to argue with you?" This was why men complained that women made no sense.

"I wanted you to *answer* me," she said.

"What was the question?"

"I said, 'There's not going to be an us, *is there?*'"

"No, you didn't."

Her eyes widened and her chest swelled as she inflated with rage. Arguing with her was the wrong answer right now. Logan prayed for calm in his own voice as he said, "If you said is there, if you asked a question, I didn't hear it."

All the storm left her in an instant. Her voice was flat. "Violet will laugh so hard when I tell her she was right."

Oh, great. Was Violet between them again? Logan was trying to figure out how they'd gone backwards when Audra flung her arms around him. That didn't make any sense either, but it was so wonderful he didn't question it. He simply held on. He was so sure he didn't want to let go that the question of marriage entered his head again. He needed to be careful not to let it pop out of his mouth. Not yet. Audra would want a speech or something.

She stepped back enough to look up at him. "Can we have lunch tomorrow to talk some more?"

"We can't talk right now?" He was looking at her mouth, but he wasn't thinking about talking.

"They're waiting for you," she said, and dropped her arms completely.

"Violet is playing for me." He brought his now free hand up to relish the soft blonde hair around her face.

Audra tipped her head to lean into his hand.

If that wasn't an invitation, then… It was an invitation. He kissed her fully until he began to feel some resistance. "What's wrong?"

She shook her head. "Nothing." But her eyes darted around to remind him that they were standing in front of her brothers' door. And they didn't need to get carried away anyway.

"Okay," he said. "Lunch tomorrow. I'll pick you up at Next Love when you're finished selling paintings."

"But then my car will be downtown."

"What if I meet you at the restaurant?"

"My second home," she said with a fond smile. "But my car would still be downtown."

"Why is that a problem?"

"I'm assuming you'll want to do something with me after lunch, too."

That was not a bad assumption, but what he really wanted was to catch her *before* she was finished selling paintings. Without having to say that. "We can talk about that during lunch."

She gave him an expression that accused him of being difficult just to amuse her, and she didn't want to admit it was working.

"So you're agreeing to have lunch with me tomorrow?" he said.

"Yes."

"And you'll say yes?"

"I just did." She eyed him suspiciously.

Logan was getting ahead of himself. He refrained from laughing outright, but he was too happy not to grin like a kid who'd learned a new trick. He was afraid the moment was turning into one of those schmaltzy times when two people who were going to see each other very soon didn't want to say goodbye. He got in one more kiss before he said it.

Audra paused, possibly to summon a bit of maturity as well, before she also said goodbye. She turned back for one last sappy smile before she turned the corner to her door on the front of the house. Sappy wasn't so bad on Audra. Logan took a moment to erase any traces from his own face before he returned to the card game.

16

*A*udra was stationed to protect her paintings. That was why she was hovering near the wall where they hung. It wasn't working. Two kids were touching her paintings while their parents discussed furniture with Elaine. Audra guessed their ages to be around eight and five, though she didn't think she was a great judge. The girl was definitely older as she was significantly taller than her brother. She was constantly proving that by touching the corners of paintings her brother couldn't reach.

The girl was moving up and down the row, reaching up to touch the work she passed while the boy followed her, jumping up and down and occasionally skimming the bottom with his fingertips. He yelled out in triumph at each touch. Every now and then, their mom would call out, "Don't touch those paintings, okay?" After the first time the kids ignored the request, Audra moved closer to her work. She hoped her mere presence would intimidate the kids into leaving her work alone. So far, it had no effect.

Several of the paintings had been knocked crooked, and Audra was dying to fix them. But she was afraid that showing the kids she wanted them straight might only give them a new game. If one of the paintings hit the floor, would the parents actually do something?

Fortunately, they finished their business with Elaine before Audra could learn the answer. They stood at the door pretending to leave without the kids for several minutes before the boy grew bored enough to leave and the girl followed him. Audra watched the door close behind the family before she got out her level and made the adjustments that were calling out to her.

"Sorry about that." Elaine's voice caught up to her after she'd checked about three quarters of the canvases.

"Not your fault," Audra said as she turned around.

"Still… we don't worry about kids in here much since most of our inventory is waiting to be refinished anyway. But I'll be sad if one of those beautiful pictures is damaged."

Audra tried to show appreciation for the concern without hinting she'd hold any of the Brachys responsible. She'd signed a waiver to that effect, but it was the personal relationship she cared about. "It did give me a chance to use my trusty level," she said.

Elaine smiled and Audra felt a shift in the conversation before she opened her mouth. "Alison tells me that you have a new understanding with the young man who was in here a few weeks ago."

The smile on Audra's face was even bigger. She'd been very happy to share that news with Alison.

"And that's why," Elaine said.

"What?"

"Because he came here." Elaine nodded with satisfaction at her explanation.

Alison was approaching from her work area, now close enough to hear. "Oh, here we go again," she said.

Audra looked between the two of them wondering where she'd lost the thread.

"It's more proof that our shop is blessed for romance," Elaine said. She put a hand over her heart and fluttered her fingers.

"Oh, right." Audra had heard something about that before.

"I think what you mean to say, Mom, is that it's another coincidence." Alison rested both hands on her hips in a stubborn posture, but there was amusement in her eyes. "Amanda's husband came here because he knew he'd find her here. Trevor only came in because his grandma tricked him. Just because Logan and Audra are moving forward after she started selling her work here… that doesn't mean one had anything to do with the other."

"How many coincidences do you need?" Elaine asked. "My ways are not your ways."

Alison just shook her head, but Audra smiled at the debate. Was it possible that God was using the shop as a springboard for romance? Anything was possible with God. And it was easy for Audra to believe when she was feeling the rush of knowing Logan would be there to see her soon. She and Alison had been trying to guess how early he would show up. She was sure he was going to come early for a painting. Would he come early enough to give himself time to talk Audra into selling him one? Or would he come at the last minute, thinking not to give her time to object?

Her heart leapt with the possibility of the earlier time when she heard the door. It was not Logan though. It was Sheila.

"Hello, ladies," she yelled across the store, waving both hands. She was wearing a fuchsia shirt and a necklace with several layers of sparkly, black beads. This was a woman who never went unnoticed.

As the three women waited for her to join them, the door to the back room opened. Alison's dad stood in the doorway until Sheila frowned in his direction. He said, "I thought I heard the door." Then he turned around and retreated to his work room again.

There was a fleeting smirk on Sheila's face. She seemed to appreciate his way of saying hello. The two of them had a weird relationship.

"What brings you in today?" Elaine asked.

Sheila patted a bag slung over her shoulder. "I sold more of those blue ones online than I expected. I'll need to collect a few I left here. Plus, I have some news I wanted to share in person."

"Good news, I hope," Elaine said.

That was a likely guess as Sheila was glowing about the news.

160

She nodded happily and brushed some hair off her forehead. There was something odd about the movement. Her jet-black hair wasn't touching her forehead, and Audra wasn't sure she'd actually moved it anyway.

Elaine prompted her patiently. "Any day now."

Sheila's left hand came up to straighten her hair again without straightening it. Audra felt her eyes widen as she thought she figured out the news. Sheila wore a lot of her own jewelry, including at least two rings on each hand. They were tiny beads on twisted wire. The one on her ring finger was different. It had a small diamond and fit the traditional image of an engagement ring.

The others noticed at the same time. Alison shared a stunned look with Audra. Elaine let out a gasp and said, "Is that what I think it is?"

"Fred just asked me last night," Sheila said. Her tone was more grateful than giddy.

Audra was trying to remember when the two of them had met. Had it been three weeks yet? Maybe four? Whatever it was, it was fast.

"That was fast." Elaine managed to say it as a simple observation, without any shock or disapproval in her voice.

"Don't worry. I'm not blinded by infatuation." Sheila eyed Alison as though she might be guilty of that and even added a suspicious glance at Audra. "Fred is a nice man. He spent forty-six years proving he knows what commitment means. That's all I need to know."

"Well, congratulations," Elaine said. "I'm sorry I didn't say that first. You surprised the manners out of me."

Audra and Alison added their congratulations as well. Sheila thanked them all and moved towards her jewelry to shift inventory. Elaine followed her, chatting about plans for a small wedding in a few months.

Once they were alone, Alison let her full surprise show as she said, "Wow. I didn't see that coming."

Audra only shook her head. She definitely would not have predicted it either.

"Oh, no," Alison said suddenly. But then she laughed so Audra wasn't terribly worried.

She asked, "What's wrong?"

"Fred came in here to look at your work."

"So?"

"That's when he met Sheila," Alison said. "My mom's going to start adding them to the list of couples she says this place brought together. She'll be even more impossible."

Audra laughed at the feigned drama of her friend. "Maybe it's actually my work that brings people together."

"I'll be happy to blame you next time my mom brings it up."

Audra pretended to be shocked even though she'd been the one to say it first. They continued some friendly banter about Audra's paintings – mostly how she'd given in and was planning another sunset as her grandma suggested – and about drawer handles. Audra would not have guessed before meeting Alison that she'd ever find drawer handles an interesting topic. But Alison had shown her so many types and shapes, and she talked about what she'd like to make if she had the tools for metalworking. Audra understood the desire to create.

All the while, they watched the door for Logan's entrance. They waved at Sheila as she left. It was only a minute later that the guy Audra had been waiting for came through the door. He nodded towards Elaine, who was engaged with a customer but smiled knowingly at him anyway.

"I guess it's time for me to go back to work," Alison said. "Let me know if anyone needs to buy a frame." Her tone was teasing, and she raised her voice enough for Logan to hear.

He nodded a greeting at her, too. He hadn't looked directly at Audra yet. There was a strange shyness as he approached, something Audra hadn't seen before.

"This wasn't the plan," she said. "We were supposed to meet next door."

Logan stuffed his hands in his pockets with a sheepish grin. "You seem to have guessed that I intended to come here first."

"Maybe." Audra shrugged. "Maybe I was hoping."

His eyes met hers tentatively, then grazed across the available paintings. "The one I wanted before is back," he said. "Please tell me it wasn't another insulting return."

She looked at the trees and smiled because she knew Logan liked it. "I haven't sold it to anyone. Yet."

"Really? Because it wasn't here... I noticed it wasn't here recently."

Rather than ask when he was there when she wasn't, Audra simply admitted the truth. "I couldn't sell it to anyone else after I refused you so I took it home. I only brought it back this morning because I thought you might... try again."

They had traveled a few steps, drawn to the painting that was their subject. Logan checked the time. It was noon and the time Audra normally left. He'd evidently chosen the no argument option. "How does this work?" he asked. "Do I have to pay for it before I'm allowed to take it down?"

"I think customers find it's easier to handle payment before they have an awkward canvas to shift from hand to hand," Audra said. "But you can have it for free."

Logan seemed concerned by the offer. "No," he said after a minute. He pulled some money from his pocket. "Your work is already worth more than you charge. I won't... um, just take it."

Audra accepted the payment with the thought that it might not matter if someday soon all his money was hers. Even in her head that sounded greedier than intended. She corrected herself that everything she had would be his at the same time.

He took the painting from the wall and held it at arm's length. "Is this the proper way to admire art?" His question was joking, but the respect with which he handled it betrayed some seriousness.

Audra chuckled at the joke and tried not to completely melt at the picture of him holding her work. For so long she had thought he was humoring her that she'd been afraid to really look. Now she could see plainly that all his words of encouragement had been genuine.

"It does need a frame though," he said.

"We're in the right place for that." She motioned for him to follow her back to Alison.

"Did you find what you were looking for, sir?" Alison asked in her professional voice.

"I believe so." Logan matched her formal tone. "Would you by chance have a frame the appropriate size for this lovely piece of art?"

"You know, I just might." Alison winked before she turned to head to the back room.

Audra was puzzled. "I didn't know she was making frames ahead of time. I thought she waited until someone ordered one."

"Hmm," was Logan's only answer.

Alison returned quickly, carrying a beautiful piece of wood. The frame was barely an inch wide, carved to look like a braided rope with bands on the corners.

"That's amazing," Audra gushed. "It must have taken you forever."

"A labor of love," Alison said with a modest smile.

"I approve." Logan held the painting out to Alison. "Would you do the honors?"

Alison nodded and accepted the painting. She set both it and the frame on a nearby table to secure them together. "Here you are."

She handed it back to Logan.

Audra was still in awe of the frame as Logan thanked Alison and began to walk away. She took two steps after him before she realized something was wrong. "Wait," she said. "You need to pay for the frame, too."

Logan smiled. "I already did."

Audra looked at Alison, who only nodded. When had they arranged this? For the moment, she decided she didn't care. She'd get the story out of Logan eventually, but right then she only wanted to enjoy the support of her friends.

Logan left the new purchase in the trunk of his car before they went to lunch. Audra noticed he had a box waiting there to protect it.

The January Café was more crowded than a typical Saturday. Ryan still appeared relaxed as he stood behind the counter where Grandma May was in the mornings. Logan and Audra found an open booth along one side. A young server named Addie came to greet them. She was an energetic brunette that Audra had been training during the week.

"Audra!" she exclaimed, apparently pleased to see someone she recognized.

"Hey, Addie. You doing okay on your own?"

"So far, so good." She smiled brightly, but it was quickly replaced with a worried expression. Addie glanced over both shoulders before she whispered to Audra. "Am I supposed to do something different for you with, um, with the check?"

Audra shook her head. "If Grandma May was here, it'd be a different story, but today you can treat us like regular customers.

Addie nodded.

"Except you can let us wait longer if you get busy."

Addie nodded again but with less certainty. She wrote down their order. They needed no time to consider since Logan knew the menu almost as well as Audra.

They had barely been left alone when Ryan stopped at the table. He looked between them, frowning slightly. "Does this mean Logan will stop being distracted on Friday nights or that you're going to spend more time interrupting?"

Audra ignored his question.

Logan said, "How's your Saturday?" which was about the same as ignoring it.

"Not bad," Ryan said. "We had a bit of a spill in the kitchen earlier, but it's all cleaned up."

"Sorry I missed that," Audra said dryly.

"Me, too," Ryan replied. He moved away as he said, "Enjoy your lunch."

"Maybe I need to get Violet next door."

"What'd you say?" Logan asked.

"Oh, um…" Audra had only muttered the thought as it occurred to her. She was remembering Elaine talking about her shop bringing people together. Ryan was there when he helped Audra bring in the paintings. Violet had never been there. But even if the place had really been blessed by God for romance, that wouldn't mean it could be used like some kind of magic love potion. Audra was only amusing herself with the thought. She would need to be subtle in her next matchmaking attempt and hadn't decided how to go about it.

"Audra?" Logan was waiting for her to stop staring into space.

She couldn't share her plans with Logan yet, and only partly because she didn't have any plans. She would have to wait until she could frame her idea to get Violet and Ryan together as wholly her idea and not prompted by Violet admitting her feelings. They would have to talk about something else on her mind. "Sorry," she said. "I was lost in thought for a minute. What do you think of, uh, my new Tichu player?"

Logan laughed at the question. "I barely met her, but I'm sure she's fine if you like her."

"Crazy that she and Cameron work together, huh?"

He shrugged. "I think it's a fairly big company."

"Yeah, but…" Audra lowered her voice. "Promise you won't tell anyone?"

"Sure."

"She introduced herself to me as Katie. That's what we were all calling her during the game. But Cameron called her Katherine."

Logan opened his mouth, then hesitated. She could tell he didn't see any significance and was searching for something to say other than so what. "I think that… isn't Katie a common nickname for Katherine?"

"Yes, but didn't… You didn't notice," Audra said. "That's actually good because I don't think you were supposed to. Anyway, right after he said hi to her, she gave me and Alison this look that seemed to beg us not to correct him. Isn't that weird?"

"Uh, not really. Maybe she prefers to use her full name at work. Maybe it sounds more professional or there's already another Katie."

Audra sighed because he didn't seem to think it was interesting.

"Oh, wait." He looked as though he suddenly understood something. "You know Cameron has some kind of online thing going on. You're not getting any matchmaking ideas, are you?"

"No." Not involving Cameron anyway. She had the impression Katie was interested in whoever wasn't coming through the door of the January Café. The name thing only added to the mystery around her new friend.

"Good," Logan said. "I think you should focus your efforts right here. Can I join you for lunch tomorrow, too?"

"Right after church?"

"Yeah."

"I guess."

"What about Monday?"

"What about it?" Audra asked.

"Lunch?"

"I'm working."

"At a restaurant."

Something about his tone of stating the obvious made her laugh. "Yeah, but if I sit down with you, one of the customers will probably think I'm rude for not getting up to get a refill or something even if I am entitled to a break. We're busiest at lunch."

He nodded. "I meant at an off time, and we could eat in the kitchen."

"That's probably not the best example for the other employees."

"It'll have to be in the evening then."

"What will?" she asked.

"When I see you." Now he implied that she was being difficult on purpose.

Audra wasn't trying to give him a hard time. She just didn't understand why he was trying to make successive plans right now when they had several free hours in front of them. "I'm sure I can see you after work. Is there a big hurry to arrange a time?"

"I just want to know I can see you each day until you're ready to commit to every day."

Oh, that was sweet. It was very sweet. And he was sitting there like he expected her to confirm an appointment or something. How could he be romantic and clueless at the same time? Audra looked closer and saw that he wasn't clueless. He knew. After years of waiting and almost talking about it, he knew how she felt about him. And she knew he loved her, too. No one had to confirm anything.

Audra let the peace of that settle over her for a moment before she said, "7:30. Same on Tuesday."

~~ The End ~~

~~ Thank you for reading. ~~

www.ingramcontent.com/pod-product-compliance
Lightning Source LLC
Chambersburg PA
CBHW051823170626
46807CB00003B/1007